the winchester house
byrne bloodline
book one

Maya Black

This is a work of fiction. Names, characters, businesses, places, events and incidents are either the products of the author's imagination or used in a fictitious manner. Any resemblance to actual persons, living or dead, or actual events is purely coincidental.

Copyright © 2025 by Maya Black

All rights reserved.

No part of this book may be reproduced in any form or by any electronic or mechanical means, including information storage and retrieval systems, without written permission from the publisher, except for the use of brief quotations in a book review.

If you would like to use material from this book, prior written permission must be obtained by contacting the publisher at:

authormayablack@gmail.com

First edition: October 2025

contents

1. Prequel	1
2. Lucia	9
3. Anthony	13
4. Lucia	17
5. Anthony	19
6. Lucia	23
7. Anthony	27
8. Lucia	37
9. Anthony	43
10. Lucia	51
11. Anthony	53
12. Lucia	61
13. Anthony	67
14. Lucia	71
15. Anthony	75
16. Lucia	81
17. Maria	83
18. Anthony	85
19. Lucia	91
20. Maria	95
21. Anthony	97
22. Lucia	101
23. Maria	105
24. Anthony	107
25. Marcus	111
26. Lucia	113
27. Anthony	117
28. Maria	121
29. Anthony	123
30. Lucia	125
31. Maria	129

32. Anthony	131
33. Lucia	133
34. Anthony	137
35. Lucia	143
36. Anthony	145
37. Maria	147
38. Lucia	149
39. Mrs. Martini	151
40. Anthony	153
41. Lucia	155
42. Anthony	157
Epilogue	159
Join Maya Black's Newsletter	161
About Maya Black	163
Also by Maya Black	165

PREQUEL

May, 2014

"Welcome to your new home, Mr. and Mrs. Yoshida," the agent said.

"Thank you," they both said, their faces beaming.

"I will quickly take my leave now," the agent said as he cleared his throat and literally ran away.

The couple looked at each other and shrugged, confused by the agent's actions.

The movers finished taking in all their belongings and then stared at the Japanese couple.

"You do know that this house is haunted right?" the owner of the moving truck said as he was about to leave.

The couple looked at each other and laughed.

"Do you really believe in that? It is just an old Victorian home with secrets, that is why they call it haunted. My wife and I have checked the house and we believe that the Winchester house is perfect for us," Mr. Yoshida shared with the mover who still thought that it was a bad idea.

"You know, we hear screams from this house every night and it doesn't sound human at all," the mover spoke again.

"It was just some broken pipes and it has been fixed," Mrs. Yoshida said before laughing as she turned around, walking in with her husband while the mover left.

"I just think saying a house is haunted is stupid. If it is

truly haunted, do they really think it would be on the market for people to buy it?"

Mr. Yoshida shook his head while his wife laughed.

"It's probably a folklore that parents told their kids around the area so they wouldn't stay out too late," Mrs. Yoshida said as she twirled around the house. "This house is beautiful. I can't wait to decorate it," she squealed.

"Yes honey, I will check if all the taps are working and we can try to arrange some of our things today and then we can continue tomorrow, okay?"

He looked at her as she nodded.

"HONEY, I think the pipe is faulty. Can you pass me the flash light?" Mr. Yoshida asked as he heard footsteps but he got no reply.

"Honey?" he said again with his hand stretched out, then he was handed a flashlight and he continued looking at the pipes.

When he was done, he went back to the living room to explain what he found.

"Babe, I noticed that the pillows were floating when I came into the living room. That is such a wonderful trick!" Mrs. Yoshida clapped her hands.

"Really? I would have loved to see that, but if you were in the living room, who would have handed me the flashlight?" He asked.

"Handed you the flashlight?"

"You didn't come to the basement to check on me?"

He had felt someone's breath on his neck and just assumed it was his wife.

"No," Mrs. Yoshida said, looking at her husband like he had grown a head.

"I felt you standing over me," Mr. Yoshida continued, but when she repeatedly asked how that could be, he dropped it.

"Ok, well, let's have dinner at that fancy restaurant we saw on our way here!" Mrs. Yoshida smiled.

"Yes, I think it is the best fit. Our gas is not installed anyway. It will be installed tomorrow," he informed his wife as they walked outside the house.

"**CHEERS** to our new beginning and our new home," they chorused as they clinked their glasses together for one last drink before leaving the restaurant.

"That meal was wonderful," Mrs. Yoshida smiled, a little tipsy from the wine they just had.

"Yeah." Her husband nodded.

"Hey, dude, are you the one that moved in recently to the Winchester house?" the valet asked him.

"Yes," he replied.

"The house is so beautiful." Mrs. Yoshida hiccupped.

"Yeah, well I'd advise you both to sleep somewhere else tonight. That place is haunted and no one has ever lasted more than a night in that house," the valet told them.

They looked at each other, then at the valet.

"Thank you for that information, but it is not really needed. My wife and I are already settled in," Mr. Yoshida said in a tone that stated they were done with this conversation and then he walked away with his wife.

They got into the car and Mr. Yoshida began to drive toward home carefully. "I can't understand what everyone's problem is, first the mover, now that valet. It is just...." His sentence was interrupted as a crow smashed into their windshield. He swerved from surprise, veering too far to the right and hit somebody's mailbox.

"Fuck," he cursed as he got out to check the damage done to his car, the mailbox, and the bird.

His wife followed him and gasped as they looked down at the dead bird.

"Looks like the mailbox is okay," she informed him after getting over her shock.

"Let's get going then," he said angrily. They settled back in and as he drove away saying, "Could this night get any worse?"

The rest of the drive home was quiet as both were lost in their own thoughts. Once they got home, they got out, glanced at each other and walked to the front door. Mr. Yoshida had the house key in his hand and reached toward the knob but the door suddenly creaked open.

"What? I locked the door," he said.

"You probably just didn't lock it properly, or the lock is broken. We will have someone check it in the morning," she said as they walked into the house.

"Oh my god! It is freezing!" Mrs. Yoshida said as she ran to turn on the heater. "It's the beginning of summer, why is it so cold in here?" she whined as goosebumps erupted over her arms.

"Maybe the air conditioning was left on." Mr. Yoshida shrugged.

"No, I turned it off," she replied.

He continued walking further into the house when he tripped on something. "What the hell? Who put that there?" He crouched down to pick up a doll.

"We don't even have dolls," Mrs. Yoshida commented as she felt uneasy. "Babe, I think we should sleep in a hotel tonight as the valet suggested," she said.

He angrily dismissed her concerns. "No, we will stay here. This is our home and don't tell me you are letting those people get into your head."

"N—no," she said quickly.

"Good." He walked upstairs and she followed him quickly.

They both got ready to go to bed but she had to do her skincare routine first. She applied her facial cleanser and opened the tap to wash it off as she squeezed her eyes closed.

After rinsing off the cleaners, she opened her eyes to see her face was red. Behind her, she saw a little girl holding a doll behind her. Blood flowed out of the tap.

"Hahn!" she screamed.

"What is the problem?!"

He rushed into the bathroom.

"T—th –the girl, blood.." she stammered out as she pointed into the mirror with shaky hands.

"What? There is no girl and where is the blood?" he asked her.

She looked down at her hands and then at the mirror and then the sink. "I –the tap…" She quickly turned on the tap but only water rushed out.

"I think you are still tipsy from the wine and you are letting these people get into your head."

"B-but I…" She looked back into the mirror at her face.

"It's okay, honey, let's go to bed," he said as he led her to bed.

"AH!" Mrs. Yoshida screamed as she opened her eyes to see the silhouette of a person looming over her.

"What happened?" her husband said as he was startled by her scream.

"There is someone there," she pointed in front of their bed as she started crying.

"No, there is no one. I think you are just terrified. You probably had a dream. We will talk about this in the morning," he cuddled her as they tried to fall asleep again.

"Ahh!" he screamed as he felt someone holding his ankle.

"Babe! What is ..... AHH!" Mrs. Yoshida screamed and jumped from the bed as she saw the silhouette fling her husband from the bed to the other side of the room.

She immediately got up and started running, her husband joined her. They heard a banshee scream and a woman with a white flowing gown stained with blood started pursuing them.

"Ahh!" she screamed as she tripped on the rug and fell down.

"Harriet!" Mr. Yoshida called out to his wife but ran away immediately after he saw the woman was already on the heels of his wife.

"AHH," he let out a deep breath as he bent down to steady his breathing when he reached the outside of the house.

He looked up to see a young man with gold teeth smiling at him and crows flying around the house, then he heard the screams of his wife and he started to run again, making his way down the driveway, not seeing the truck until it was too late.

"GOOD MORNING, everyone. It is really sad as we record another death in San Jose. Mr. Yoshida, aged 34 years, and his wife, aged 32 years, were found dead this morning. Mr.

Yoshida was said to be running when he got hit by a truck, while his wife was found hanged to death on a tree close to their home. May their souls rest in peace," the news reporter said.

 # LUCIA

May 2024

"Welcome to your new home, Mr. and Mrs. Martini," the agent said to them.

"The house is beautiful," Mrs. Martini gushed as she stared at the Winchester house.

"Yeah, it is," Mr. Martini smiled at his wife.

"I think it needs to be repainted," I said as I studied the house through my thick rimmed glasses.

"It's yours, you may do as you wish. I will quickly take my leave now," the agent said as he cleared his throat and literally ran away.

"I would advise you to run and leave this place immediately. This house is haunted, nobody lasts for more than a day here. You need to leave or you might be recorded as the next dead person in San Jose," the mover warned as he drove off.

"What does he mean by that?" I said, looking amused. "And I thought my stay here would be boring!"

I smirked at my parents who just ignored me, as usual, and walked into the house.

As I walked into the house, I saw them as they stared back at me. They seemed to be glued to the wall.

"Hi guys," I waved at them but they didn't respond to me.

They appeared to be studying me.

"Who are you saying hi to?" Mother asked me as she looked at the wall and back at me.

"I am talking to those people. They are weirdly dressed."

I chuckled.

"Who?" My mother said, looking at me weirdly.

"You can't see them?"

I was confused.

"See who?" she replied again.

"Them!" I pointed at them, feeling frustrated.

My parents looked at each other and then back at me again.

"Have you stopped taking your medications?" my father asked.

"I do not need my meds. I am not depressed!" I said to my parents.

"Dear child, I am not saying you are depressed but you need to take your medications," my mother softened her voice as she lightly touched my cheeks.

"Okay, Mom," I replied as I wondered how my life would have been if I wasn't out with my friends that night.

I waited until my parents walked out and then I walked towards them.

"You do know that I can see you, right?" I asked them, laughing.

Then the little girl moved towards me with her creepy doll and her tangled hair that seemed to be covered in blood.

"What happened to you?" I asked her as I took a deep breath, assessing the injuries at the back of her head.

"You are rude. You didn't even ask me what my name is," she said in a little voice and looked away like she was hurt.

I decided to play along with her as I crouched down and smiled at her.

"I am sorry. What is your name?" I asked her.

"My name is Madeline and I was killed in the backyard. My step mother had enough of me and my sister and she pushed us from the balcony. My sister found peace and went to the afterlife but I decided to stay back and torment my step mother. I enjoyed every piece of it and I killed her," she said looking at me with doe eyes that I didn't fall for.

I looked at her for longer and she moved closer to me so she could hold my hand.

I stood still and continued to watch her as she held my hand and smiled at me.

It wasn't a cute smile. It looked like I had seen the true face of evil and she suddenly started to chant something.

I quickly removed my hands from her and she lost concentration, staring at me like I had done something bad to her.

"Not today, sweetheart."

I laughed and walked away.

ANTHONY

I woke up this morning feeling anything but happy. I was very tired and very irritated. Partly because of the annoying ghost I had to deal with last night and because she appeared in my dreams again.

"Hello, dear."

Mother smiled at me but I didn't feel like returning the smile, so I walked towards her and hugged her instead.

"Good morning, Mom," I said, walking to the kitchen island.

"Why that sulky face? You see her again?" she asked me.

"No, well, yes. She appeared but she isn't the main cause of my annoyance."

I sat down and took a sip of my coffee.

"The ghost from yesterday, that is," I continued.

"I thought as much. She was really loud and asked a lot of questions," Mother said, and I just grunted in reply.

"Ha, I just knew he'd be mad this morning," Lucien said as he took his laptop from the coffee table and headed to the door.

"See y'all later today."

He saluted us and left.

I sighed.

Sometimes I wished my life was as simple as his, since he really didn't have many responsibilities, unlike me. I have to head the Byrne Ghost Hunting Inc. and still worry about our hotels and resorts.

"Hey, sweetheart," my father kissed my mother's forehead and moved into the kitchen. "He still mad from yesterday's ghost?" he asked my mom.

"Yeah, she was pretty annoying, taunting him with all his painful memories and then he dreamed of her," my mother filled my father in.

"Hmm. I think he needs a break," Father shrugged.

"And he is here, and leaving."

I stood up and left.

I loved my family but sometimes they can be extremely annoying.

I looked at my mail, then I showered and put on my new Armani suit and walked out of the house.

You might be wondering why a thirty-year-old man is still living with his parents. Well, let's just say I have my own penthouse in New York, close to our company's headquarters, but I still love spending time with my family anytime I can.

I walked into the Bryne Resorts and Real Estate headquarters and I noticed all the staff rushing to get busy.

It's funny how they gave me a nickname, Mr. Grumpy. I promise I am not grumpy. I am just not in the mood to smile stupidly half of the time.

"Good morning, Mr. Bryne, we got a new intel on the land you sorted out last week. It is available and up for sale," my secretary informed me.

"What is the price that it was listed at?" I asked as I continued to walk to my office with him behind me.

"It is two hundred thousand dollars for three plots," he responded.

"I will take it at only one fifty. I know they are selling because they need the money and the land has lost its value. Tell them one fifty or nothing," I told him as I walked away.

"Okay, I will do that," he nodded.

"MOTHER! Why did you book a vacation without asking me? I am attending a fundraiser that week," I complained.

"You need to unwind, you have been extra grumpy lately." Mother always ignored everything I said.

"I do not need to unwind. I will not be following you all on the vacation," I threatened.

"Anthony Sebastien Bryne! You will do no such thing!" she raised her voice.

"We will see, Mother," I held my laughter knowing I would follow them on the vacation but I just wanted to make her agitated.

"Anthony!" she screamed.

"Okay, Mother, I was joking." I laughed.

"I have idiots for sons," I heard her complaining to my father before she hung up the phone.

I quickly called my brother.

"Damien, what are you doing in Spain? I need you at the headquarters tomorrow. We are going on vacation at the end of the week. I need to close certain deals this week and I need you to help me coax one very annoying ghost to the afterlife," I explained to him.

"I am having the time of my life and no, I cannot come back anytime soon. I am busy with ...."

"Damien," I heard a lady moan.

"Just don't get anyone pregnant and I want you here by Thursday," I said to my playboy brother before ending the call.

"Anthony," Lyra walked into my office.

"Hi, boo," she said, sitting on my desk.

"Lyra, this is not the time, I am busy," I said to my girlfriend.

"I just found out that you are going on a vacation without me," she whined.

"It is a family vacation, Lyra," I said tiredly.

"So, you mean I am not family?" she asked.

Why am I even with her? How did I start dating her?

Honestly, I could have never seen myself with a woman like Lyra five years ago and after the incident with the woman that haunts my dreams, I am very sure that I have no feelings for Lyra but I can't just break her heart like that.

I really need to tell her that I don't have feelings for her.

 # LUCIA

"Ahh!" I heard my mother scream a few nights later as she ran out of the bedroom.

Father and I were in the sitting room. "What happened?" he asked as he stood up.

I watched as the ghosts laughed and I saw Berry coming down the stairs. I had found out that the only ghost I could talk to, or that would talk to me, was Madeline, and she was still trying to kill me even though I could tell that she enjoyed talking to me.

"I saw a woman in a wedding dress in the mirror when I entered the bathroom," she said looking very scared.

"I know we have been experiencing abnormal activities. I mean, last night when I came down to drink some milk because I couldn't sleep, I saw the pillows moving around in the air and one floated towards me," he informed us.

"Yes, there are ghosts in the house," I said to my parents who turned to me with wide eyes.

"Ghosts?" she asked.

"Yes, ghosts. There are five of them to be precise, that I've seen so far. They are the people I saw when I first came into the house. I can't talk to all of them, only Madeline. She told me that she died in the nineteen hundreds and she wanted revenge and she has been living here ever since," I explained to my parents.

"Th –that's impossible," she stuttered.

"What do you mean there are five ghosts living with us?" he asked, looking at me like he was finally understanding what I was saying.

"I can see them," I said.

"Are you not taking your medication again, honey?" she asked me as she took a step towards me.

I took a step back.

"I am taking my medication and I am not just making up things. I have a feeling you don't believe me."

I looked towards Madeline.

"Show them that you guys are here," I told her.

She had a mischievous glint in her eyes as she ran towards my mother and bit her before kicking my father's legs.

"Ouch!" they both screamed at the same time and ran behind me.

"Is there any way they can leave?"

I looked at Madeline and back at him.

"No, they can't, or won't," I said to my parents.

"Alright, can we share and will they agree to not torment us?" she asked.

"They want us to leave and the only reason they haven't killed us yet is because I can see them," I said exactly what Madeline said as chills ran through my body. At the same time, I was thrilled.

My mother gasped, threw her hands up in the air, and shouted. "There is no way I am going to leave this house for them. I love the house and I am staying!"

They all stared at her and at that moment, I felt fear flow through me as I noticed the murderous glint in their eyes.

They will try to kill my mother, I know it.

ANTHONY

"I can't believe you guys decided we needed vacation in Australia!" Lucien complained for the hundredth time.

"Lucien, please, I am jet lagged. Stop being a baby and suck it up." Christian walked past Lucien into the bedroom.

"How are you people not complaining? This country is dangerous. It is filled with poisonous animals and kangaroos. What is there to love here?" Lucien shouted in frustration.

"Please, stop, you are making my ears bleed." Christian walked into the living room again.

"I cannot believe..."

"Hey!" Lucien shouted as Christian slapped the back of his head.

"Shut up, man," he responded.

"Boys! I will not have you guys fighting in my living room," Mother said sternly as Lucien stood up to hit Christian back.

"I don't understand why you are fighting. This place is beautiful and we are close to the beach. Our house is literally on the beach," Damien said.

"More reason to be scared. There could be sharks or sirens in that water," Lucien commented.

Christian shook his head.

I stood up and walked out of the room. I have had enough of their drama and now I want to get back to work and vanish my disturbing thoughts.

"ANTHONY, please don't leave me, I love you," she cried as I walked towards my car parked on the other side of the road.

"Anthony, please," she cried as she ran after me, not seeing the truck moving towards her until it was too late.

"Ahhh!" she screamed.

I turned back in horror to see her lying lifelessly on the ground.

Almost immediately, I saw her spirit staring at me with tears flowing from her eyes.

My heart hurt and my head felt too heavy.

I had just watched the love of my life die.

"Isabel," I called out.

I opened my eyes.

"It was just a dream," I breathed out but it was more than that. It was a daily reminder of how I had lost the one woman I would have done anything for.

I let out a deep breath and stood up from the bed as I walked into the bathroom.

I have to get out of here.

"What some cinnamon toast?" my mother asked.

"No, I am not hungry," I said as I walked out of the house.

I felt choked.

I needed to breathe.

I walked along the beach as I allowed myself to think of everything that happened that day.

My breath hitched as I saw a silhouette floating on the water.

"Fuck no, I am not doing ghost duty on vacation," I cursed as I walked back to the house.

"Hey, boys, do you all want to go on a boat cruise?" Mother asked with all smiles.

"Hell yeah, I need that," Damien said while Lucien looked at Mother suspiciously.

"Why do you want us to go on a boat cruise?" he squinted his eyes at her.

"Nothing serious, I just want to spend more time with my family," she shrugged nonchalantly and I knew something was up.

"If you don't give me the real reason, I will not go along with you." Lucien stared at Mother.

"Okay fine, I found out someone drowned here last week and the spirit has been disturbing the fishermen. We are actually here to send her to the afterlife," Mother confessed.

"Hell no, I am not doing that on vacation," Damien said as he turned away.

"You all are coming along with me. This ghost is really mischievous and it's on water. Anything can happen. Plus I need your wits and we haven't gone on an operation like this in forever. It is also very dangerous for me and your father to go alone," Mother said, looking at us with doe eyes.

"Fuck!"

"Damn!"

"I guess we are all going then." I shook my head and Mother showed us her perfect pearly white teeth.

Mother can be overbearing sometimes.

I had a lot of work to do and she has known for a while that I am not interested in any kind of ghost hunting. I am always reminded of Isabel and the ghosts have been more annoying lately.

"Mother! I cannot believe that you booked a cruise boat just because you wanted to track down a ghost!" Lucien exclaimed.

"It is a vacation, we have to enjoy ourselves obviously."

Mother rolled her eyes like Lucien had asked a stupid question.

Damien and I made eye contact and shook our heads. We decided to enjoy ourselves since we are on vacation and had been out here for hours.

"I see her!" Christian said, alerting all of us.

"Okay, looking at her, can you tell us any backstory?" Mother asked him.

"She wasn't drowned as people believe. I think that is why her spirit didn't go to the afterlife. She was strangled to death by her abusive boyfriend," Christian said.

You'd be surprised by the number of ghosts that are killed by their partners because of some argument.

"Okay, so this is the plan. Lucien, you will try to track her trail. I know it is harder because we are on water but you will have to find a way. Christian, continue to get more information on the events that led to her death. Anthony, you will talk to her to find out why she is still here, who hurt her and promise her to make the person pay for it. Finally, Damien, you will coax her and lead her to the afterlife," Mother informed us.

"What will you be doing, Mother?" Lucien asked.

We all rolled our eyes even though what he said was right. Mother is the best ghost hunter among all of us and she has special abilities, but since she retired, she left everything to us. She prefers to sit and watch.

"And what about Father?" Damien asked.

"He is in the cabin resting," she smiled at us and walked away towards the cabin.

"I can't believe this. They brought us to work but they are on vacation." Damien shook his head.

 LUCIA

It's been three months now and the ghosts are getting more violent. Berry has tried multiple times to kill Mother. The last time, she possessed Mother and took her to the rooftop so she could jump down and kill herself.

I pleaded with Madeline, who made me buy her a lot of candy, not that she could eat it.

"I am tired of all this already!" Mother screamed.

Marcus kicked her leg and she crouched down, moaning in pain with pure rage on her face. "What the fuck!" she stared at me and my father like we were the cause of her pain.

"Honey, stop annoying them and they will stop bothering you," my father suggested to my mother, who looked at him like he had just said the most stupid thing she had ever heard.

"Can you hear yourself? I should stop annoying them? They are the ones annoying me! We literally bought this house and it was very expensive and you expect me to leave? Never! I will make sure they leave! Even when I didn't do anything to provoke them, what did they do? They went into my kitchen and shattered all the contents in my fridge, and mind you, they were all perishable goods! I will make them pay," she said and stormed away.

I walked upstairs and went to research more on ghosts and reasons why they can remain in the house. I knew something for sure. They wouldn't tell anyone their story and I am very sure they didn't know each other's story either. I was determined to find out what happened to each and every one of them.

My mind screamed that it was a bad idea but I think they are good people overall and that they only started possessing and killing people as a defense, and for revenge, as Madeline said.

That night, I decided to buy a Ouija board.

"I am telling you, Cat; it is a whole lot. Sometimes I wake up to them watching me sleep and I can tell you that it is creepy as hell," I told my best friend, Catherina, who was currently exploring Italy, about the psychotic ghosts I live with.

"I am so glad you don't feel I am mad. My parents felt I was seeing things at first because I told them about the ghosts. They started believing me when they started getting disturbed by the ghosts. Now my mother annoys them and they are determined to end her life," I said to Cat.

"I believe you because I can see them too," she whispered to me.

"For real?" I gasped.

"Yes, I went to one lady here in Italy for a spiritual cleansing and the opening of my third eye and what I have experienced since the cleansing, I cannot explain it," she confided in me.

"Woah, that's really crazy. Is it weird that I am fascinated by the fact that I can see them? I just bought a Ouija board," I said to Cat.

"Girl! Are you for real? One thing my mama told me is that I should not fuck with anything that is spiritual and I take that seriously. The spiritual cleansing I went for that has gotten me into trouble was a drunken dare. I had to go with Rina because I was dared, not because I wanted to," she explained.

"I am just curious," I replied.

"Alright, sweetie, whatever you do, please be careful. We will continue our discussion later, I've got to go," she said. We said our goodbyes and ended the call.

ANTHONY

"Mother, I think we need to go to the shore now. It's already too late. I think the water gets more dangerous at night. Don't forget the sirens will be watching too. They would want to see what we are up to and the ones that are not so nice will try to enchant us all," I said to my mother as the ghost mysteriously disappeared.

My brothers and I have been trying to get hold of our little ghost friend. I think she noticed we were following her sometime in the mid-afternoon and she decided to disappear or hide.

"I think I can see her," Damien said instantly.

"Where?" Lucien asked as he tried to track her trail.

"Behind that rock," Damien pointed to some weirdly shaped rock just at the left side of the beach.

"Hell no! I cannot and will not be following you people towards that rock," Christian spoke firmly.

"Why?" Lucien countered.

"Because, it has a lot of sharks around it and that is the siren's rock. There is no way I will be going towards that rock and that is final. You guys can drop me at the shore and come back over here," Christian repeated.

"But we need more information about the ghost," Damien argued.

"Her name is Grace," Mother interrupted and we all turned to face her.

"How long have you known?" I asked her, getting slightly annoyed.

"Since we set our eyes on her," she shrugged.

"And you didn't think to tell us, Mom?" Christian looked at her.

"I'm sorry, loves."

She blew air kisses at us.

We all shook our heads and continued our ride back to the shore.

This is something Mother usually does. I guess that is why I am not surprised. She loves seeing us struggle to get the job done, even when she knows that we are clueless on what to do and she knows ways she can give us a head start.

"Come on, my babies, you all shouldn't be angry at me. You know I just really love seeing you guys work together and that it's to make you stronger." She looked at us like we were bullying her.

"Mother, we would have still worked together and the case would probably be solved by now if you had given us all the information you knew." Lucien shook his head and we all looked at mother in agreement with what he said.

"IT'S BEEN two days and the ghost hasn't been on these waters. Do you think she has migrated somewhere else because she thinks we are looking for her?" Christian asked.

"No, she's probably still around. Do you remember ten years ago when we went on that dangerous case in London that the ghost was very angry and displeased and us showing up made her angrier? I think the situation is similar," Damien said.

"Come on, boys, don't be discouraged. I have an idea on how we will catch her but first we need to spend some family time together. What do you think of going downtown for a nice dinner tonight?"

Mother smiled at us.

"Finally, we get to do something I like," Lucien cheered and we all agreed.

"I am so happy that I can spend this amount of time together with my babies!" Mother started crying.

"What is going on, Mom?" I held my mother's hand, feeling worried.

"I just.. you all were drifting apart and I couldn't bear it. I just love seeing you boys together and working together. It makes me happy. I could have solved this case alone with your father but I wanted you all to bond. My dear boys, I want you to understand the importance of family and working together is the best way." She smiled at all of us.

"Ughh! You just really know how to make us do your bidding. We had no choice anyways." Lucien rolled his eyes while Mother laughed.

"Yeah, that's true. We are actually enjoying this. I don't remember the last time I was with you all together in the same room or when we were eating dinner together," I said looking at my brothers.

"I HAVE FOUND information on the ghost!" Christian said excitedly the next morning as we all sat on the breakfast table.

"Really? What did you find?" Damien asked while we all looked at him expectantly.

"Okay, so I researched all the women with the name Grace

that came here for vacation within the last month, which I suspect was the time frame in which Grace was killed, and I was right. I found a woman with exactly the same frame and hair as the ghost we found walking on the sea. Her name is Grace Donovan." He stood up and ran upstairs. He came down with his laptop.

"Look, she came here with her boyfriend and went missing about two weeks ago. He reported her missing and they found her body in the sea."

He showed us her details.

"Okay, how can this help with our hunt?" Lucien asked, still not getting Christian's point.

"We know she was strangled and thrown into the water, but her autopsy suggests she was also raped," Christian continued.

"Well, now we fully understand why her spirit would still be roaming looking for vengeance," Damien added.

"I have an idea," I spoke up instantly.

"Let's go to the sea now and Christian can check the hotel she was staying at with her boyfriend before she went 'missing'," I said as I added air quotes to *missing*.

"She was at the Seaside Hotel. It is on the other side of the beach," Christian responded to me after checking for the hotel.

"Just as I guessed. Now it all makes sense why she would be roaming around the sea and I can tell you just where she would be," I looked at all of them and they understood instantly.

"Okay, but we need a plan this time or she will disappear again," Damien said, reminding us of what happened when she saw us the last time.

"Okay, we will work like this. We need to find out when her boyfriend left and what caused him to kill her. Then we need to find her and talk to her. We need to know her actual intention on the reason why she chose to remain here. We need to understand her line of thought. Then we will find a way to convince her to go to the afterlife and we will find evidence to make sure her boyfriend ends up behind bars," I said to my brothers.

"I will hack into the airport's database to check who she came with and her boyfriend's name, although from what I am seeing here, I think they came from Argentina." Lucien stared at Christian's laptop.

"Okay, I've gotten into the airport's database," Lucien rejoiced after typing furiously for about fifteen minutes.

"His name is Roberto Fernandez. He is from Italy but he lives in Argentina." He then searched up information about Roberto.

"Guys, you need to see this," he spoke up but his eyes were still glued to the screen.

We all gathered at his back as we looked at the laptop.

"Grace is not his first victim, she is just the first lady he has killed," Christian repeated what all we had just read, out loud.

"So, we are dealing with a rapist and an abuser who has been to jail four times in the past three years," Damien said.

"How does he keep getting out of jail? We need more information on him to find out what is actually going on." I looked at Lucien who went back to digging out more information.

"His brother is a lawyer," he responded to my question in five minutes.

"The hell?! Now I know why he has the audacity to continue abusing women," Damien spat out angrily.

"The last woman before Grace was abused so badly, she ended up in the psychiatric ward," Lucien continued.

"What do we do? He will get out of jail again if we provide

evidence against him and we may not even be taken seriously. I mean his brother is a lawyer and all of this happened in a different country from where they live," Lucien asked.

"We will find a way to lure him out. We have to catch him in the act so he will be sanctioned in a country where his brother has no right to act and he will definitely be sent to jail," I spoke with finality in my tone.

People like him infuriated me.

"Okay, good. Now that is sorted, we need to call Amelia to meet him in Argentina," Damien said and we all nodded in agreement.

"Now we have a ghost to catch," I smiled at my brother and we walked down to the boat.

"Oh my God! Grace, no!" Lucien shouted as we reached the other side of the beach to see Grace trying to drown a kid.

She stopped and turned to look at us. She started fading away when we stopped the boat.

"Don't you dare, Grace," I spoke in a tone full of authority.

"What do you want from me and why can you see me?" she said in a whiny voice.

"We want to make a bargain with you and we hope you can stop disturbing this body of water," I spoke to her.

"And why will I stop? Do you even know why I am here?" she asked as her eyes flashed in rage and I almost groaned out loud. Dealing with angry ghosts was like dealing with toddlers.

"Obviously, we know why you are here. If not, we wouldn't be speaking to you. You need to listen," I said in the calmest voice I could muster.

"We have to speak to you on some matters. Will you be kind enough to give us an audience?" Damien threw her his most charming smile.

"Hmph!" she huffed as she floated towards us.

When she got close enough, she stared at us and asked, "What do you want to say?"

"Why didn't you go to the afterlife like other spirits?" Lucien asked this time.

"I want to meet somebody; I have tried going home several times but I cannot because I am stuck here. My body was buried here and I really just want to go home," she shrugged and started fading away. I quickly threw our spring towards her and it wrapped around her arm making her bound to me.

"Let me go," she said trying to remove the spring from her but it wasn't going to work.

"Tell us the truth, why are you here?" I asked her more sternly now.

"I am here because I want to take revenge on someone. He will be here by this time next month with another woman and I will be able to kill him and gain eternal peace," she said, her eyes turning from blank to red to indicate her rage.

"Can you tell us details on the last events before your death?" Damien asked.

"Roberto and I came here for a vacation, or so I thought. I noticed some weird things about him and I found out he was cheating on me with another woman who was back home in Argentina. I confronted him and things got heated. He used his tie to strangle me, then he raped me and threw me in the water. I was already out of breath and I was bleeding from various injuries. I couldn't swim. He watched me drown," she explained to us.

I knew it was a watered-down version of the story she gave us because I could see her last memories from being bound to her by the spring. Chills filled my body with a murderous intent.

I will make sure that fucker ends up in jail, or better still, dead. The world didn't need people like him.

"We can promise you that we have made arrangements to make sure he ends up in jail and we just want you to be at peace. You being here is disrupting the balance of this world and every day that you are angry, you have a lot of energy and you release it on to anything on your path. You are causing harm to everyone around here. Please, will you go to the afterlife and we promise to handle this for you," Damien said gently.

"No! My life was cut short! Everyone deserves to suffer like I did. I am not going anywhere!" she screamed in a shrill voice.

No, not again. I cannot be faced with another peaceful soul being turned into a monster.

One thing my family and I have realized is that when these ghosts stay in our world too long with a murderous intent, even the most gentle one among them could become very dangerous and cause havoc that will affect innocent lives.

"We do not want to force you, please leave," my mother said sternly now as she came down from the boat and walked towards us.

My mother walked with a certain kind of authority that brought a chill down our spines, like it always does when ghost hunting.

"You don't want me making you leave this world."

My mother smiled at her in the most unhinged way.

"I... you... no! I need to take my revenge!" Grace screamed desperately as she felt my mother moving closely towards her.

We could all feel it. My mother had opened the portal to the afterlife.

"We will take care of Roberto. He won't hurt anyone again, and if he tries to get out of charges because of his brother, he will meet you in the afterlife and you can spend eternity hating on him and trying to kill him out there. Now, I will say it one last time. Go into this whirlpool now while you can or I will make you, and trust me, it will be very painful.

Your soul would be scarred," Mother spoke in a very spooky voice.

I had goosebumps.

"I will go, but you have to give me your word that Roberto will pay!" She stared into Mother's eyes. Mother stared back at her and nodded.

"Of course, he will pay dearly." Mother smiled at her.

She nodded and walked into the portal that Mother had made between our world and the afterlife.

"Good bye, Grace," Mother called and the portal closed.

We all turned and stared at our mother.

"You know we could have done that, yeah? You didn't need to show up or show off." Damien faced Mother with a scowl.

"I know, but I got bored of watching you guys and this was already taking up most of our vacation that I very much still intend to have." She turned and walked away, leaving us staring at each other.

"I am mad that Mother didn't let us end the case. Something tells me she just wanted to watch us struggle to see if we still had it in us to handle the case," Lucien confirmed all that we knew.

"Yeah, but let's look at the bright side. We get to spend the rest of the vacation in peace."

Christian smiled and then Mother walked back in with a scary grin on her face.

"I knew it was too good to be true. There is no way we were going to have a good vacation that was full of relaxation," Lucien said angrily.

"What makes you think we cannot continue our vacation in a haunted house?" Mother looked very excited, like a child with their favorite candy.

"Mom, can you hear yourself? Vacation in a haunted

house? And I am being told you aren't a psychopath." Damien shook his head.

"Damien Alejandro Bryne! I will not allow you to speak to your mother like that," Father defended Mother as he came around the corner.

"Okay, I am sorry!" Damien raised his hand to show that he was not trying to offend my mother.

 # LUCIA

I sat on the floor with the candles that I had purchased along with the Ouija board. I had researched how to communicate with the dead. They claim you have to be partly psychic and you have to make sure you don't summon some other spirits that are not meant to be there.

I lit the candles and noticed that Berry stood in front of me. After I moved the sage around, I began asking my questions.

Normally the way a Ouija board works is that the letters on the board are supposed to spell something for me but instead, Berry was actually responding. I could hear her voice; it was raspy and kind of soft.

I felt scared but at the same time I was very excited. Her voice left goose bumps on my hands.

"Why are you still here?" I asked her.

"Because I want to take my revenge on the man that murdered me. Look at me, I am still in my wedding dress. I had a wonderful life and he robbed me of it. Now I will make sure to kill everyone that steps in this house." Her eyes turned red and my candle lights began to flicker off, one after the other.

I suddenly felt chills down my spine as I became scared.

Why the fuck did I decide this was a good idea?

Berry picked my legs up and started to drag me out of the room.

"Help!"

Madeline appeared in front of Berry.

I couldn't hear their conversation because they weren't moving their mouths, just their eyes.

"Why did you try to talk to her?" Madeline asked me.

"I... I just wanted to know her story," I stuttered.

"You made her angry. Part of me wants to teach you a lesson for not listening to me!"

These ghosts were now mad at me, so it was no longer thrilling, just downright scary.

"Please, I am sorry," I begged as tears started to fall from my eyes.

They ignored me as Berry dragged me to the basement.

There was no one else at home.

I should have listened to Cat, now nobody can save me.

I am going to die.

As we got to the basement door, I already had a few injuries from being dragged from upstairs down to this point.

"Lucia?" Mother called out.

"Mom!" I screamed as the tears continued to flow freely from my eyes.

"Lucia!" she called again; this time I could hear panic in her voice.

"Mom, I'm in front of the basement!" I cried.

I heard her running through the hallway towards me.

"Oh my God, my baby," she gasped as she sat beside me.

"What happened?" she asked as she took in my wounds, my disheveled hair, and the tears streaking on my face.

I held my mother and I started sobbing.

"I.... I ... t–tried. I wanted to speak," I choked on my words and couldn't speak anymore. I just continued sobbing but I am sure Mother understood because she became angry.

"This is it, I have had enough. You all can do anything you like but trying to harm my daughter is where you have crossed the line," Mother shouted angrily at the air, not knowing where they stood.

I saw them all look at me and smile and I knew that this was the beginning of my problems.

"Mom, let's just leave. They will try to kill us," I said in fear.

"No, this is my home and I am not leaving. Instead, they will be the ones that will be leaving," Mother spat out in anger.

I did not go back to my room. I spoke with my mother in the living room until my father got back. She narrated the entire thing to him.

"Oh, Lucy, you should not have tried to talk to them. Now they are angry and we don't know the lengths they are willing to take." My father hugged me, bringing me some comfort.

"We will sleep in a hotel tonight," he said and I nodded.

"No, we are not going anywhere. Those ghosts will have to leave my house tonight. They have no idea what an angry mother can do," Mother responded.

"Honey, we cannot stay here. They tried to kill Lucia. What makes you think they won't try to kill us all while we sleep?" my father asked.

"I'd love to see them try," Mother replied as I saw them file into the room with psychotic smiles.

My mother had challenged them.

Mother did everything to make me feel comfortable. That night after dinner, I refused to be in my room alone.

"Mom, Dad, can I stay in your room tonight?" I asked in a small voice.

"Of course, darling, there is no way I will allow you to stay by yourself after all you have experienced," my father said and I sat on their bed.

It didn't help that I could see them and their reactions. It made everything scary, and I just wanted to run away from the house.

I should not have tried to talk to Berry.

My family has never been religious but that night I wished we could say a little prayer before going to bed.

At exactly midnight, I heard giggles. I opened my eyes and looked at my parents to make sure they heard it, but they were asleep.

I must have imagined it.

I closed my eyes to go back to sleep.

I heard giggles again but this time a melody followed. I opened my eyes and this time I could see a little silhouette standing at the foot of the bed.

I was sure it was Madeline but I was so scared because I already had made her angry.

"M..m..mom.." I lightly tapped my mother as the melodies grew louder.

"Hmm?" she answered sleepily.

"Can you hear that?" I whispered.

"Hear what?" she answered.

This time the melody continued but it sounded far away, like it wasn't from our room.

She heard it. I felt her body stiffen.

Just when we thought things couldn't get worse, Berry appeared and this time my mother could see her, too.

"Ahhh!" Mother screamed and I shook in fear.

"What is going.... Jesus Christ!" my father exclaimed as he saw Berry stepping towards our bed with her neck positioned in a very weird manner.

"I will give you only five minutes. Leave this house now or I'll kill all of you and your bodies won't be found," a very low chilly voice said, but Berry's mouth did not move, making me feel a greater fear envelop me.

"We are not leaving. Be ready to put up a fight with me

because you are not touching my family," Mother spoke defiantly.

"Your wish," the voice said, then laughed.

"Mom!?" I called out to my mother as I started crying.

I didn't want to die now and even if death was to come, certainly not like this.

Blood started to trickle from the ceiling and when I looked up. I saw a dead woman's body pinned up there.

I screamed and jumped off the bed alongside my parents.

Mother opened the drawer close to her bed quickly and took out some leaves that were tied together and a lighter.

She lit it up and instantly the room was filled with a scented smoke and Berry started to scream. She disappeared and everything stopped. The dead woman on the ceiling was no longer there and everywhere was suddenly calm.

"What is that and where did you get that from?" my father asked my mother.

"I went to meet my new Haitian friend today and she gave it to me. She told me it was sage and I should put it in whatever room I am in. When burned, it will cleanse the air, and the ghosts won't be able to stay wherever it is," Mother explained.

"Okay, but wouldn't that make them even more angry and make them try other means?" I asked.

"Yes, that is why we will call the best ghost hunters in the world to help us get rid of them." Mother smiled and took out her phone.

ANTHONY

Ever since Mother had told us that we were going to a haunted house, Damien had been smiling in the most unhinged way.

"What is wrong with you, bro? Why are you so excited?" I asked for the hundredth time as we flew back to America in our private jet.

"I don't know anything about being in a haunted house and dealing with more than one ghost excites me!" He laughed.

I shook my head. "You are so weird."

My other brothers laughed at us.

"Mom, where exactly are we going?" Christian asked.

"We are going to the Winchester House," Mother stated with a smile.

"What?!" we all said in unison.

"Multiple people have died in that house," Lucien said.

"Yes," Mother responded.

"Mother, seriously, that place houses the most dangerous ghosts!" Damien said.

"Not ghosts we can't handle." Mother shrugged.

"Plus, it will be fun," Father added as we just stared at each other.

Fun?
I don't think so.
A shitload of work?

Yes definitely!

"This is crazy," Lucien said as the chauffeur picked us up and drove us toward the Winchester House.

"Do people even live in this house?" Christian asked.

"Of course! What do you think? That we will go to an empty haunted house?" Mother jokes.

"Not putting you both past it," Lucien said to my parents and they just chuckled.

"Wow, the house is big and scary as hell. I don't know how this family has been living here for three months but based on what I have read, no one has been able to stay in the house before for more than a night," Christian told us as he continued with his research.

"The lady that employed us told me that her daughter can see them. That is why they didn't disturb them at first but then she..."

"Annoyed them by trying to communicate with them," I finished for my mother who just nodded.

"Except, she could already communicate to one of the ghosts. She just wanted to talk to all of them," Mother continued.

"That family must be crazy because there is no way I am walking into a haunted house and deciding to live there after I have seen ghosts."

Damien laughed.

"We will understand their line of thought when we get there," Father said.

We all sat in comfortable silence until we got to the house.

"Woah, it's actually beautiful," Christian said as he got out of the car.

"Yes, it is," Mother said, then we all spotted something.

A little girl with a creepy doll that waved at us.

"That is a ghost," Lucien said.

"Is she here to welcome us? Because now that is creepy, even for me," Damien added.

"Hopefully not," Christian said and we laughed.

"Hello? Mrs. Martini, we are here and standing outside your door," Mother said over the phone to whom I assumed to be the owner of the house.

A lady walked out of the front door to meet us.

"Hello," she greeted us before she smiled.

"Hi, we are the Bryne ghost hunters, owners of the Bryne Ghost Hunting Inc.," Mother introduced us.

"Oh…" the woman seemed speechless at the fact that the entire family was present.

"We were on a vacation when you called so we decided to continue our vacation here," Mother explained further.

"Oh, that's wonderful."

"Mom?" I heard a voice call out. I looked towards the door to see the most beautiful girl I have ever seen in my life.

Damien hit my back in a subtle manner and whispered in my ear, but I am sure my other brother caught it because they snickered.

"Stop staring at her like you want to eat her," Damien whispered.

I almost slapped him back but I realized we were outside and Mother would not approve.

"Shut up!" I whispered harshly.

"Lucy, these are the ghost hunters I told you about earlier today. They will handle the issues we are facing," Mrs. Martini said to her daughter, who nodded while looking at us.

"Hi, um, my name is Lucia." She waved awkwardly at us like she just realized she was supposed to say some type of greeting to us.

"Hi," we responded in unison, making Mother and Mrs. Martini laugh.

"You all should come in." Mrs. Martini opened up the door.

"Hell, no," Lucien said as we entered the house and saw the ghosts standing on the staircase railing as if welcoming us.

"You can see them too, right?" Lucia asked and we all nodded.

"That's about seven ghosts. I see why this place is known to be haunted," Damien jokes.

"There is something wrong. I mean I cannot get through to them. It's like there is a blockage."

Christian groaned because he knew this meant it will take longer.

"They have been ghosts here for a very long time. They feel like they own the house and they see us as a disturbance. They don't want us here. I can feel their energy," Mother said.

We walked into the sitting room and we took our seats while Mother asked them some questions to know the full extent of what has been going on.

"How have you stayed here for three months without considering you could have called us before?" Mother was intrigued by the fact that they lived so long with such violent ghosts.

"They liked me, at least Madeline did, but she got angry when I tried to speak with Berry," Lucia explained.

"What do you mean by they liked you?" Christian asked, shocked.

"When we got here, I saw them all and I tried to say hi to them but they didn't respond. Only Madeline did and we have been talking for a while and I asked her why I couldn't speak with the others. She told me it was because they weren't in the mood to speak," Lucia replied.

"So, you went against her and tried to speak with one of them?" Damien questioned.

"Yeah."

"Wow, you are really brave. It is a shock you are not dead yet. Normally ghosts don't like being disobeyed, especially territorial ghosts like the ones you have here," Mother explained to them, although I could tell they already learned that the hard way.

"Mom, the ghosts have disappeared." Lucien looked spooked.

"No, they only dematerialized. I can still feel them, they are here," Mother explained.

"This is not normal. Nothing about this is normal." Lucien looked around and I knew from his look that he couldn't see their trails.

This will be one very tough ghost hunting.

"Let's get you all settled in and then we can find a way to proceed with this ghost issue."

Mrs. Martini smiled warmly as she showed us to our rooms.

I really don't know how the Martinis have been staying here for so long. The place had the air of death and was really cold. I felt uneasy and it wasn't something I could brush off.

That evening we all had dinner in the dining room with the Martini's. Lucia wasn't very conversational and only spoke when she was questioned or someone spoke to her.

"Stop ogling her!" Christian whispered harshly into my ear but Damien by my other side heard it because he snickered.

I stomped both of their feet and Mother looked at me with stern eyes. I am very sure she heard everything and she knew what was going on, even under the table.

After dinner, we all tried to make a small conversation and Lucia was the first to stand up.

"Good night, everyone." She smiled at us and we all said it back and she left.

I wanted to go with her, to talk to her at least. She is so quiet.

"ANTHONY, DON'T LEAVE ME," she cried.

"Please stop crying. I could never leave you," I begged and when she looked up at me, she was faceless.

I gasped as I opened my eyes. I saw a silhouette standing at the foot of my bed. Most people would have been scared but I have been through worse.

"What do you want?" I questioned the figure.

"Take your family and leave. This is no place for you," she said trying to sound intimidating but she only made me laugh.

"What is your name?" I asked her.

"Berry," she answered.

"Who killed you?" I asked another question.

"My father-in-law wanted his son to get married to his rich friend's daughter. We were in love and he couldn't handle it. On my wedding night, he pushed me from the third floor. When I landed, I was still alive but he proceeded to smash my head with a statue. I can still remember the pain I felt. I promised myself that I would get my revenge," Berry said to me.

"Have you gotten your revenge?" I asked.

"No, the fucker died in a car crash and his son refused to live in this house. My soul has been lonely since then and no matter how many lives I torment, I am not satisfied," she spoke truthfully.

"I understand why you are angry now. You never got the revenge you deserve because the man you'd swore to haunt died prematurely. You hate it that he got peace and you didn't," I spoke to her and for the third time in my life, I saw ghost tears.

"But do you realize you are in so much pain because you refuse to let go? If you are willing to let go, I can lead you to peace," I comforted her. "I can lead you to the afterlife," I said calmly.

She looked convinced for a moment but in the next second, her eyes turned red and I knew she was about to let all hell loose.

"No!" she screamed in a shrill voice and ran towards me and leaped on to me, but I was quicker and moved out of the way.

I took out my cuff from my bed and pinned her hands to my bed post.

"Ahhh!" she screamed and everyone ran into my room to see Berry pinned to the bed.

"What's going on?" my mother asked with fear in her voice as she moved to check that I hadn't sustained any wound from how violent Berry is.

"We need to calm her," Father said as we all looked back to Berry, who was thrashing against the bed trying to go out.

"She is really hurt, I can feel her emotions. It is full of rage," Lucia said, surprising all of us.

"You can make her calm," Mother said quickly, voicing out all of our thoughts.

"How?" she asked, confused.

"Make yourself calm," I answered.

"Okay," she nodded and took a deep breath.

 # LUCIA

I tried to focus on my breathing to calm down but it was becoming harder and harder. I started to choke. It felt like someone was holding on to my throat.

Black spots began to fill my vision as I felt myself sway back and forth.

"She's choking," I heard someone say.

I opened my eyes and it felt like I would lose my breath again. The person that was holding on to me was Anthony. He was very handsome with jet black hair and gray eyes.

"Are you okay?" he asked me.

I nodded as I pulled out of his arms and stood properly.

Berry smiled at us and then she stared at me for a while. There was something hypnotic about her eyes because it felt like I could get lost in it.

"Stop, Lucia, don't look at her. She is trying to bond herself with you," someone shouted as Anthony walked in front of me.

"What was that?" I asked, suddenly feeling confused.

"I don't think it worked," Anthony said to everyone.

"I have opened the portal to the afterlife, Berry. You have to get in now," Mrs. Bryne said.

"I will not go. You cannot chase me from my home," Berry responded angrily.

I didn't understand why but I suddenly became angry that they were trying to send Berry to the afterlife.

This is what I want right?

So, why am I mad that they are about to send her to the afterlife?

"Ahhh!" Berry screamed in pain and soon, I too, started to feel an intense pain.

"Ahh! Stop that!" I screamed at the top of my voice.

"Hell no!" Lucien shouted as he kicked the bed while Berry smiled.

"She bound me?" I asked in a scared small voice. They all looked at me with pity and nodded.

"She doesn't want to go, so she bound to you because whatever she feels, you will feel it too, and if she gets pulled into the afterlife, you will follow," Christian explained to me.

"You mean death?" my mother asked and they nodded.

Nope, there is no way I am dying young.

I shook my head.

ANTHONY

Mother suspected that Lucia would be able to help us find whatever Berry was looking for since she was now emotionally connected to her.

We decided to start our search from the basement because it made more sense as we found out that Berry spends most of her time in the basement.

After three days of searching and not finding anything that was worth anything, we decided to search somewhere else.

"Let's look through the attic," Lucia said.

"That place is way more creepy, and I don't think I want to be involved in looking for a ghost's item in the attic," Lucien said.

We all nodded in agreement.

But we have to find the item.

We tried entering the attic but we found it was sealed off with a material so solid, we could not break it down. We needed a device that would be used to blow up the door.

We were still discussing different ways in which we could enter the attic when the little girl appeared.

"I think you all should blow it up. We really want to see inside," she said.

"You all can't go inside either?" Christian asked and she nodded.

"Well, now we know this door was intentionally built to

hide something from the living and dead," Damien said and we all grunted in agreement.

I moved forward to check what the door was made from. I had a few guesses but I had to call Michael to know if it was truly what I thought.

"Do you know what it is?" Mother asked.

"I can take a guess. I'll be back," I walked downstairs.

"Michael," I said as soon as he picked the call.

"Yes?" he responded.

"Your last assignment, the door that guarded the house and trapped in the ghosts, can you send me a description? I think I have found something like it," I said.

"I'll email it to you now," he responded.

I opened up the email and compared the details to the door in the attic. It was eerily similar.

"This is surely a Teflon door. To break it down we will need to use the same device that Michael and his team used," I informed my mother.

"Okay, I will make a call to have the device shipped now," Mother said.

Over dinner, we were all discussing the turn of events and it occurred to me that Berry is likely the oldest ghost here and is keeping the other ghosts together.

"I think we can send all the other ghosts away if we send Berry away first," I said to everyone seated on the dining table.

"Yes, that's my theory too," Damien agreed with me.

"Thank goodness, the package is here already," Mother exclaimed in joy as she opened up the delivery box.

We took the blaster and fixed it to the Teflon doors and took cover while Lucien excitedly pressed the explode button.

The door burst open and we walked inside. The attic looked like some kind of shrine.

Lucia launched forward and went to the back of what looked like an altar and took out some kind of Ruby stone.

"This is what Berry is looking for, this is her lost item," she said calmly but her eyes had some kind of shine in them.

"What is that?" Christian asked as he collected the stone from her and stared at it in amazement.

"It is a birthstone," Mother responded and we walked towards the room where Berry was bound.

Berry was no longer thrashing against the bed and she looked relieved to see us.

"Why were you looking for this birthstone?" Mother asked.

"Because it is mine," Berry said.

"Okay, good. Now you can go peacefully into the afterlife right?" Lucia asked.

"I need to be buried with it," Berry responded.

"Where is your grave?" Mother asked calmly.

"I don't have one. I was thrown into the ocean to rot," Berry replied. I felt for her.

"We can have a bargain. We will host a funeral for you and you will move to the afterlife?" Damien suggested.

"Yes, I am okay with that," Berry agreed and I released a breath of relief. Some part of me thought she would reject it.

We arranged for Berry's funeral that night. The following day, we had her buried properly with her birthstone and she agreed to go to the afterlife.

The other ghosts were easier to persuade to go and soon we had sent them all to the afterlife.

"Ha, another job well done," Christian sighed as we planned to go back to our jobs and everyday lives. Then we sensed a sudden chill that flowed through the house.

"What was that?" Lucien asked.

"I don't know, but I felt it. Did you feel it too?" I asked my brothers.

"Yes," they all responded and our mother came running downstairs with everyone.

The look on their face said they felt it too and this wasn't like anything we had experienced.

It had the chill of pure evil.

"AHHH!" We heard the chilling scream coming from upstairs as we were setting the dinner table and we all ran to see what it was.

Mrs. Martini was the only person upstairs. She was in the bathroom.

We walked into the bedroom and saw a message written in blood and a crushed skull on the bed.

"THIS IS JUST THE BEGINNING," It read.

"What the hell is this about?" Lucien said.

"I think something more evil and powerful was locked up in that attic," Mother said. Even though we had been hunting ghosts all our lives, we were afraid.

"I DON'T UNDERSTAND why wouldn't you like that restaurant. I think it is...

What I was saying was cut short as we walked into the house. We met five people sitting on chairs with their heads twisted at an odd angle.

The living room suddenly felt very cold and we felt shivers go down our spines.

"We have been dropping warnings but you people do not

listen," the big guy sitting in the middle said as he stared at us with his blood red eyes.

We all stood at the door not knowing whether or not to fully come inside or stay outside.

"Who are you?" Mother asked.

"We are the Legion and we are the souls of the altar that you disturbed," another one answered.

"Disturbed?" Lucia answered.

"You broke into our home in the attic," they responded together.

"You don't belong here. Your home is the afterlife," Father said.

"Hahahahaha," they all laughed together.

"We are not like the others. We are different."

The man stood and everything in my body screamed to run, but before I could make any moves, we were drawn inside and the door shut.

I **WAS BACK** in that penthouse. It looked too small and she walked towards me.

"Hi baby, welcome home," she smiled and tried to hug me.

"You are not meant to be here, you are dead. I led you to the afterlife myself," I said.

"What are you talking about?" she asked.

"You are dead, Isabel. This is not real!" I shouted and she started to cry.

"You want me dead? I thought we were in love?" she asked me.

"I love you, Isabel. I still do, but you are dead," I said suddenly, not understanding what was going on.

"You killed me! You killed me, Anthony!" she cried as she walked towards me, blood flowing out of her eyes.

"No, Isabel, no," I repeated moving backwards until I was trapped by a wall. "Isabel, I didn't try to kill you. I never wanted you dead, you know that. It was an accident," I tried explaining to her.

"No, Anthony. You wanted me dead and now, I will kill you too!" Her eyes became red and her teeth elongated, her nails became sharp as she moved towards me.

I couldn't move. I saw a hand hold me against the wall. I tried to struggle but the hands were so strong.

I tried to scream but another hand clasped my mouth, silencing me, while another held my throat.

Isabel was already so close and smiled in a very cold manner.

She dug her fingers deep into my chest and I screamed as I felt pain like I have never felt before.

I opened my eyes quickly and I saw the faces of people I have never seen before.

Their faces were shaped weirdly. I wanted to say something but I found myself drifting back to sleep.

I SCREAMED, opening my eyes to see myself surrounded by my family members.

I took in their stares but I was trying to remember something.

"What happened?" I tried to stand up but pain instantly gripped my entire body and I shouted.

"Mother, look. He is bleeding." Lucien pointed to my chest and I looked down to see a pool of blood.

"What the fuck?" I removed my shirt and found fresh claw marks on my chest. My mind instantly went to her.

"Anthony! What happened to you?" Mother asked, looking alarmed.

"Isabel. Isabel attacked me. Mother, something is wrong. There are people in the .... " I screamed as something with a very large head appeared before my mother and tried to eat her head.

"Mother, watch out!" I screamed but they all looked at me like I was going crazy.

"I have brought the..... " Lucia screamed, pointing to my mother's head.

"Mrs. Bryne, your head!" she shouted at the human-like creature that was salivating at my mother's head.

"What are you both talking about?" Mother and everyone turned around, but didn't see anything.

The creature smiled at us and disappeared.

"You saw it, didn't you?" I asked and she nodded. Everyone looked at us like we were crazy.

Something was definitely wrong.

 # LUCIA

"What creature are you talking about?" Mrs. Bryne asked us.

"I cannot explain what it looked like. It was kind of human but with animalistic features," I explained.

"First, we need to clean up Anthony's wounds. Something weird is going on," Mother said as she brought out the first aid kit.

"What do you mean Isabel did this to you, Anthony? She is dead," Damien said.

"She came to my dream. She blamed me for her death. She turned feral and I tried to run but was held back. She clawed at me and when I opened my eyes, I saw faces that were shaped weirdly. My eyes were heavy and I closed them, then woke up shouting to see myself surrounded by everyone," Anthony explained.

"This is really strange. You both saw a creature standing over me?" Mrs. Bryne said.

"Yes," we said in unison as we nodded.

"I think it has something to do with the attic," Anthony said.

"Yes, that's true. I felt I was being watched last night. When I opened my eyes, I saw a shadow but then it was gone," I said to them.

"I have been having a strange feeling of unease," Christian added.

"I think there is more to this house than we know and we need to get to the root of this problem," Mr. Bryne said.

"Remember the warning we received? We have unleashed something. They called themselves Legion."

Anthony shook his head.

"I think I remember something," I said and everyone turned to me.

"I usually heard some cries at night when we first moved to the house and I thought it was the ghosts. But Madeline told me something that made me change my mind. She said it was the locked ones," I explained.

"What did she mean by that?" Lucien asked.

"I don't know, but there must be a connection between them and this room because how is it that only Anthony is affected? And how can only them see creatures?" Damien questioned.

No one knew the answer.

Every day weirder incidents occurred and there was no explanation for it.

Anthony got crankier because of the disturbing dreams he was having of Isabel, who happened to be his ex-girlfriend.

I got up one morning and I had the urge to search my room. I felt like something was hidden in my room. I didn't know why but the urge was driving me crazy and I had to call my mother to join me.

After hours of searching for God knows what with no new leads, Mother tried to get me to stop searching but I couldn't. It was like being possessed by something and I had to find it. I went through my closet many times, tapping every inch of the wall until I found it.

I ran towards my cabinet and came out with a small blade that I used to cut open that part of the wall.

"Found it!" I smiled triumphantly. I pulled out what

looked like a journal and Mother stared at me like I had gone mad.

"How did you know that would be there?" she asked me.

I just shrugged.

"I don't know. I just had the insane urge to go through my room for something. Although, last night I felt like I saw a lady hiding something in my room."

Mother's eyes widened.

"I hope we have not bagged more trouble by getting this house. Why are we just experiencing all of this?" Mother said, then she looked at me again.

"Why do you have a blade in your cabinet, Lucia?" She looked at me accusingly.

"Mother, it is not what you think. I was not planning on harming myself. I have had this blade for a very long time," I reassured her.

"Please don't repeat what happened. I don't think I can go through seeing you lying lifeless again. If you don't feel too well, please tell me," she pleaded as tears filled her eyes. I felt sick in my stomach.

"Mom, don't worry. I know better than to try and end my life," I smiled at her.

Are you sure?

Do you really know better?

A small voice in my head asked me. I ignored it and changed the topic.

"Let's check out what this journal is all about," I said to my mother.

"Why don't we call the Brynes first and tell them what we found," she suggested.

"It doesn't matter, Mom. It's a journal," I tried to persuade her to look at it first before telling the Brynes.

The journal belonged to a woman named Maria. She built this house with her husband. The first few chapters I read are about how she and her husband decided to build the house and how their lives were going. I thought it was just a story of a woman's life and how her life was until it turned.

Her husband was in a voodoo cult and that was his altar in the attic. But that wasn't all.

When I fell asleep that night, I saw people trying to warn of what was to come. I wasn't the only one who saw them.

"WHY DIDN'T you tell us you found a journal?!" Anthony griped at me.

"I thought it was a harmless book! How did I know it was going to intertwine our dreams?!" I shouted back.

"You really don't see what you did wrong? Why are we dreaming of the same thing?!" he asked as he ran his fingers through his hair in frustration.

"I don't know," I replied in a quiet voice.

"Okay, enough of this shouting. We need to understand what is going on and find a solution," Mrs. Bryne spoke calmly.

"This wouldn't have happened if *some* people were smart enough to know that there are *some* things you need to show the ghost hunters first." Anthony eyed me.

"First of all, this is my home, and secondly, you could have told me.. that you found another journal. But you kept it to yourself. I did the same but you are blaming me because things are going south," I retorted.

"You have no fucking right to talk to me like that! You and your family dragged us into this mess. I am the one getting dreams of the woman I loved torturing me while you sleep soundly at night. You are the one that caused a problem with

Berry the last time. You are doing it again because you are stupid and don't think!" he shouted.

The room suddenly felt too small. The room was packed with people all staring at me. It felt like they were laughing at me.

I did the next thing that felt right to me. I turned around and I ran away. I ran out the front door and didn't stop until I was far away from the house.

ANTHONY

I don't know why but something about Lucia started to annoy me. Seeing her in my dreams was a lot because I was still dealing with the loss of Isabel, even though I didn't want to admit it. It didn't help that I was attracted to our employer's daughter. That wasn't part of the plan.

Part of me felt I had that reaction to Lucia because she kind of reminded me of how I felt when I first met Isabel, but that is not quite true.

Normally, my dreams would be horrible and I dreaded going to sleep, but last night it wasn't bad at all. In fact, it was the most pleasant dream I have had in a while but that was what irked me. I was extremely disturbed that she was in my dreams.

I felt bad when I saw the look on her face before she ran out. I should not have said what I did. Everyone was staring at me like I was a villain. Mother shook her head because she could not fathom why I acted like that to Lucia.

"How dare you talk to her like that?" Mrs. Martini spat angrily.

"I... "

"No, I don't want to hear it. Just make sure my daughter comes back to me whole. You weren't here last year when she was so uninterested in life and I found her lifeless body in her room. You weren't there to feel what I felt. You weren't there when I cried every night that she was in rehab or when I had to plead with her to take her medication every night. Now she is finally doing well and interested in something and you talk to her like that. What gives you that right?!" Mrs. Martini shouted.

I took in her words and it felt like a bucket of cold water over myself. If I wasn't feeling any remorse before, I was definitely feeling it now. I felt like an asshole.

"Calm down, honey. We need to go after her," Mr. Martini said to his wife. She stopped throwing daggers at me with her eyes and ran outside with her husband.

"Why did you talk to her like that?" Damien asked me.

"I don't know," I sighed as I rubbed my temple.

"Normally you keep your cool during situations like this. Was the dream that bad that you had to lash out?" Lucien asked.

"No, it wasn't bad. I just didn't appreciate the idea of Lucia in my dream," I replied with frustration.

"This discussion can be continued later. We need to find Lucia," Mother said and we all walked out of the house.

After hours of searching, we finally found her in the park sitting by herself. Her mother started walking towards her but I stopped her and begged her to let me go by myself.

I was the one who caused this mess, so I will solve it myself.

I walked towards Lucia.

"Hey," I said as I sat beside her.

"Hi," she said in a small voice.

"I'm sorry for the way I spoke. I haven't really been in a good mood but that it is not a good enough reason for me to act like an asshole," I apologize to her.

"I'm sorry, too. I mean I should have told you guys about the book. I really don't know what I was trying to prove by keeping the book to myself," she said quietly.

"It was not your fault. You were only trying to understand

things. I should have said something about the journal I found too," I said.

"Hmm, yeah."

She shrugged and I stared at her for a while, then I chuckled.

"What's so funny?" she asked.

"It's just funny with all of the weird things that are going on that we can be all dramatic like this." She nodded.

"Are you ready to go back now? Our families are waiting for us," I told her after a while.

She stood up and we walked back together.

 LUCIA

"Maria is talking about something hidden in the floorboards. We have to take a look," I said to everyone as I walked into the sitting room.

We realized that there were multiple journals from Maria and Marcus. They are not related to each other as their journals date to different times, but it is giving us some kind of insight as to what is going on.

"What do you think is hidden in the floorboards?" Lucien asked me.

"I don't know, but if there is anything I am learning from this book, it's that her husband was an evil practitioner and whatever we are experiencing now is an aftermath of his poor choices," I responded.

"Okay, where exactly are we to look?" Damien asked me.

"I think it is here in the sitting room," I said and we started moving around the tiles to see if there was a loose one.

"I think I found it!" Lucien declared excitedly as he tried to remove the tile while we gathered around him.

He finally removed it and found a sack hidden in the little hole.

He brought out the sack and opened it. Inside, we found a necklace.

"It was Marie's protection necklace, according to what I read in the book."

"How does this help or improve our search?" Lucien asked as he set the necklace on the table.

"I don't know," I said after studying the necklace for a while.

"What did the necklace protect Maria from?" Father asked.

"It protected her from whatever her husband was conjuring up in the attic," I responded and suddenly it clicked.

When Maria died, she wasn't with her necklace. Whatever killed her could have come up from what her husband had conjured.

"In one of Maria's journals, she wrote that she had misplaced her necklace and that she had been having a lot of lucid dreams. She would wake up with marks on her body," I said remembering what I read.

"It is possible that whatever killed her must have come from the attic," Anthony finished up.

"Could it be that somebody wanted Maria dead? But then how did you know about the floorboards? Maria was the one that wrote about it. Wouldn't that mean she was the one that hid her necklace in the floorboards?" Damien questioned.

"I think it was Marcus that hid the necklace in the floorboards. I don't think he lived in the house at the same time as Maria. He got here after Maria and her husband had died. He even mentioned seeing Maria's ghost once," Anthony said.

"It doesn't make sense. I mean, there is a possibility that Maria's ghost is locked up somewhere in this house," I responded.

"What do we do now? All of this is messy," my father said.

"I think we need to start in the attic," Mrs. Bryne said and I shook my head.

"I don't think I would like to venture into the attic," I spoke up immediately.

"Same here," Anthony agreed with me.

"What is going on? Is there something we know nothing about, but you do?" Christian asked and everyone slightly nodded.

"We won't be going to the attic because we have both seen the horrors the attic holds," Anthony said.

"What do you mean by the horrors the attic holds?" my mother asked.

"Okay, how do I explain this? Do you remember when we said we saw a creature by mother's head?" Anthony said and everyone nodded.

"What does that have to do with the attic?" Mr. Bryne asked.

"We are getting there," I responded.

"Do you remember the feeling of unease we all felt that night?" I asked and they all nodded.

"The spirits called the Legion believe their territory is the attic, thanks to Maria's husband, who used that place as their altar," I explained.

"Berry's birthstone wasn't meant to be there and I can't help but think that we made a mistake by opening the attic," Anthony continued.

"Why?" Damien asked.

"Because these spirits are pure evil. There is something about them that brings chills to my body. Anthony and I have felt their presence many times in our dreams. When we wake up, it looks like we were being watched in our sleep," I replied.

"How is this happening to only the two of you?" Lucien asked another question.

"That is a question we can't answer," Anthony said.

"It's crazy how you both were at each other's throats and now you are completing each other's sentences," Christian laughed.

"They are acting odd," my mother chipped in. I threw a glare her way.

"What? I am just saying," she raised her hands and shrugged.

I just shook my head.

"Somebody has to go to the attic," Mrs. Bryne said and we all nodded.

My father and Mr. Bryne volunteered to go. Lucien opted to at the last minute.

ANTHONY

Today was the third day that we tried to go to the attic. For some fucked up reason, no one was able to enter without running back out.

"It is becoming concerning. What are they seeing in the attic? Why are they running out so fast?" Lucia asked me.

"I really don't know. They refused to talk." I shook my head.

"I think we should go together. It looks like whatever is in there breaks them. Haven't you noticed all their weird behaviors after coming out of the attic?" Lucia said.

"Yes, but are we going into the attic right now?" I questioned.

"Yes," she held my hand and we walked into the attic.

We both gasped when we looked in. It looked exactly like our dream, except the faceless people had faces and they were staring at us.

"We were waiting for the both of you," they all smiled at us.

"Why?" I asked them.

"Only you both can fully understand our ways," they responded, but their mouths didn't move.

I looked at Lucia. She heard too.

"Who are you people?" Lucia asked.

"We are the Legion," they replied.

"No, who are you? Truly, who are you?" she asked.

"We are spirits that refuse to leave your world," they answered.

"Why are you here?" I asked them again.

"We are here because Maria summoned us," they responded.

"Where is Maria?" Lucia looked curious.

"We are getting to that," they explained.

"I know you have questions and they will all be answered, but you have to follow us," they said. I looked at Lucia, who looked at me and nodded. We walked together still holding each other's hands.

We followed the Legion to a beach. It looked like some bonfire party.

We looked around and then noticed the woman singing. It was Maria.

"Maria was a musician?" Lucia whispered.

"Yes, one of the best," they answered and we moved to another scene. This time, it was a hospital. Maria gave birth to a baby boy.

"But her journals said her husband sacrificed...."

"Wait, you'll see," the Legion interrupted Lucia.

They took us back to the attic where Maria uttered some foreign words, began to move in circles and slit her baby's throat.

Lucia moved back in horror.

The Legion showed us the truth regarding Maria. In her own sick universe. She said was a good person and it was her husband that committed all the crimes, but she had no husband.

Her journals were a lie and it made me wonder if Marcus's journals were too. But he came here after Maria was killed and he wasn't a ghost hunter. Apparently, he knew a few tricks and locked Maria's ghosts somewhere in the house.

"WE NEED TO TALK," Lucia told everyone as we ate dinner.

"What do we need to talk about?" her mother asked curiously.

"What did you see in the attic? I have a feeling you all saw different things. We need to know that. From what the Legion told me and Anthony, Maria's journal could be a lie and we need to work together to find out this mystery," Lucia addressed everyone.

"Okay, I will go first," Mother said.

"I was looking up in a room with different ghosts. They tormented me. I could not send them to the afterlife and that frightened me," Mother spoke and I understood what she meant. That was every ghost hunter's worst fear.

"We were trapped in the middle of the sea. We didn't know our bearings. We kept on seeing strange faces and we couldn't make out what they looked like. We were tormented by pure evil," Lucien spoke for himself, my father and Mr. Martini.

"I found Lucia drowned," Mrs. Martini said and I realized something.

"The attic was showing you all your fear and you were living in it," I said to all of them and they nodded.

"I think if we want to get anything done, we need to go in together," Lucia stood up from the table.

The lights flickered off.

"What is going on?" I heard Damien whisper.

The room became very cold.

Then we heard footsteps.

"Who is there?" Mother called out but received no response.

Lucia came close to me and whispered in my ears. "Maria."

The lights suddenly came on and were way too bright. My eyes hurt and I had to close them.

Then the light dimmed.

"Whatever you are, stop playing with the lights," Mrs. Martini shouted. The lights came back to normal. It looked like nothing happened.

"What the hell just happened?" Christian asked.

"Look," Lucien pointed to the staircase.

"The trails. They lead upstairs," he looked at us.

We all stood up and walked behind Lucien as he traced the trails. They led to the attic.

"Maria," I called out.

"Oh, hello. I didn't mean to scare you guys," she said in a nice tone.

She moved closer to us and I spoke up, "Stay back, Maria. Why are you here?"

"My shrine," she giggled.

"You practice voodoo? Your journals said your husband..."

"What about my husband? I just wrote that so nobody would find out and I can cover up my tracks." She shrugged.

I suddenly felt a chill and unease settled in my gut. Something was not right about her.

I knew she was violent and there was something else that made me want to recoil and run from her. Her feelings, it was different.

She was no ordinary ghost.

"Welcome to my home," she smiled at us. I felt a shiver run down my spine as goose pimples appeared in my arms.

We left quickly before deciding to go to dinner to talk away from ghostly ears.

"THERE IS something off about her. I don't know what but I can feel it and it is making me uneasy," I told them in the restaurant and Lucia agreed with me.

"She has an evil essence around her," Lucia said.

"I think she is just a normal ghost that was locked away and she wants to go to the afterlife," Christian shrugged.

"No, she wants to stay here. She already claimed the house as her home," Lucia responded to Christian.

"I think we should stay away from the house for now. It is dangerous to go in," Mother said as everything dawned on her.

"What? But that is my home," Mrs. Martini said.

"We know, Mom," Lucia replied.

"We are not saying we should abandon the house. I just want to see Maria's true intentions. We need to leave for at least a week," my mother explained to the Martini's.

"If we stay the night, trust me, she will try to kill us. She wants to raise a Legion army," I spoke.

"She has been angry and trapped for years. She has grown stronger and she is waiting to release her wrath on whomever she can. If we let her, we will all be dead before we know it," I added.

"Where is Marcus's journal?" Lucia asked me and I brought it out.

She turned to the last page, looked at it, then turned it around. She stared at it for a while and said to us, "The last page is missing."

"We will get the last page later but not right now," I replied.

That night. we stayed in one of our resorts in the state. In the morning, we got back to the house and found it arranged in a different way.

Maria was nowhere to be seen and we took the things we needed quickly and left the house.

# LUCIA

"I am tired of this. I need to go home!" my mother complained for the hundredth time today.

"We will go home soon, Mother. We need to get more information on Maria. Christian is on it," I tried to calm her down.

"Honey, you have to be calm. We don't know how violent Maria can get. From what we have heard, she could just be pretending," my father said to my mom.

"I just want our home back," she spoke quietly.

I knew how attached my mother was to the house. She had wanted her own house for as long as I can remember. And just when things were finally going good, we just had to choose a ghost house.

MARIA

It feels good to be back again. That stupid Marcus locked me up but not before I made him write my journals. I wanted them to be my biography one day.

I am finally free because people came meddled in my attic. I just need to make a few adjustments and I will have my home again.

I know they gave me space because they want to find out more about me, but I already took care of that years ago. They wouldn't find anything about me except for things that I created myself.

They will be back and I will be ready.

I smiled.

ANTHONY

Almost two weeks have passed and we still haven't found anything about Maria. Something tells me that she knew that we would find nothing about her and we would have to go back.

Lucia walked into our apartment at the resort and her eyes instantly met mine.

I smiled and walked towards her. "Hey, found anything new?"

"No, but my mother is very restless. She has been saying that she wants to go back to the house. I feel scared," she whispered to me.

Since our argument and the dreams we have been having together, we have gotten closer and can easily confide in each other now. What amazes me is how I easily want to comfort her whenever I see her stressed. I don't know if it was her presence in my dreams but Isabel decided to rest and has stopped disturbing me.

I held her hand and squeezed lightly, "Everything will be alright. We will find a way to cleanse your house and your mother will have her home back," I reassured her.

"I think found something!" Christian shouted.

We all ran to where Christian was. We hunched over him as he typed rapidly on his laptop.

He turned to us as he said, "Maria strategically put everything about her out here in the world. If we are going to ever find out anything real about her, we will have to go back to that house regardless of the precautions we may want to take. Luckily, she wasn't so secure about others... because I found a file about Marcus. It is not open to the public and it took me a very long time to find it. I think Marcus was possessed by Maria. I don't think Maria was the one that wrote her journal. I think Marcus did. The reports say he killed himself and although there is a really high chance that he is already in the afterlife, I really doubt it. I think Maria had something to do with his ghosts. That is how they are intertwined. All my research says that Marcus was the next person to stay in the haunted house after its owner, Maria DeLaurenti, passed away."

I nodded a lot. It felt like I was taking in information I already knew but I didn't care to think about it or admit it to myself. I looked at Lucia and the look on her face told me she already knew, too.

She turned back to my brother. "That means we are going back to the house," she stated.

"The sooner the better." My brother nodded.

"Okay, let me inform my mother." She turned and quickly left.

"I think someone has gotten over Isabel and is now into Lucia," Damien teased.

"Shut up," I said but a grin broke out on my feigned stoic face.

"Are you in love with her? Or you are still figuring out what you feel?" Lucien asked me as they all sat around me trying to pry information out of me.

"I don't know. I will say I am still figuring out what I feel for her but I know she makes me very calm," I answered honestly.

"I thought she used to irritate you? How did you suddenly start tolerating her? And having feelings?" Christian asked.

"I honestly don't know. All I know is that her happiness matters to me and I don't want her feeling sad. I like when she is talking to me but at the same time I don't want it to look like I like it. I don't know. It is something I will figure out with time, I hope."

"You are whipped, bro," Damien said.

They all laughed but I knew what he was talking about. I felt fear grip me.

That night, I could not really sleep, even though I knew we had a long day tomorrow. I was tossing and turning and thinking about this thing I feel for Lucia.

Does she even feel the same way?

Will getting closer to her cause her more harm than good?

I kept questioning myself because I knew she had already been through so much. I couldn't just let her fall in love with me without knowing what it could cause her. If she even felt the same way.

I finally got some sleep at dawn before my alarm woke me up. In just under two hours, we were driving back to the house. Lucia sat beside me and held my hand tightly.

What if she saw me as emotional support only?

We got back to the house and Mrs. Martini was very eager to go inside. I saw the change in her features when she realized the house had been rearranged.

"Welcome home," Maria appeared with a very creepy wide smile.

"Why are you still here? You had the opportunity to go to the afterlife. Why didn't you go?" Mother asked her.

"Something about the afterlife seems boring, don't you think? I didn't want to die. I was brutally murdered. I was researching how I would get another body for myself. The world must know who Maria is!" She sat down on one of the chairs.

Suddenly, I realized something. "You sacrificed your son to

the Legion because you wanted to remain here after your passing. You knew you were going to die and you sacrificed your child because he was a bastard baby. That is why there is nothing about you getting pregnant in your journal," I said.

She looked at me for a while in surprise before she started clapping and laughing.

"You are so smart," she said like a proud mother. "You know many people wouldn't have been able to guess that?"

She rested her back on the chair.

"You created the Legion. You went to the afterlife before. You found them and bound them to you!" Lucia gasped when she finished.

We all turned to Lucia because of what she said. We looked back to Maria.

She laughed and responded, "Why do you all look shocked? What if I did? I knew I never belonged to the afterlife and my journey there proved it. That place is so damn boring and there is no way I will spend eternity there." She rolled her eyes.

While we were talking, I felt a new presence among us. It was the Legion. But something in their faces didn't look right.

They didn't want to be here.

"Maria, you need to release the Legion and send them back. You are messing with the world's balance and have been for centuries," Mother spoke seriously.

"So?" Maria asked nonchalantly as she checked her nails.

We walked upstairs, away from Maria. We didn't think staying in separate rooms would be best this time. We took off the door separating the two rooms so Maria wouldn't be able to get in.

"We need to get some protection and something that will make her not be able to come in here. This room should be only for us. We can do that, right?" Lucia's mother said.

"We can and will. I will send for some materials. We will

need to line our walls with Teflon. That is the one thing ghosts or spirits can't go through and we will add a reformer. They won't be able to listen to us," Mother explained to us.

I sat down close to Lucia. I could see the exhaustion etched on her face. I wrapped one of her hands in mine as she laid her head on my shoulders and took a deep breath.

I was sure we were thinking the same thing. That we just wanted this nightmare over with.

LUCIA

The last few days in this place have been very depressing. Maria was everywhere except our room and we couldn't stay in the room all the time because of the Teflon made the room stuffy. We couldn't open windows either, or they'd be able to hear us and enter the room. It made us all on edge.

I started taking my medications again. I noticed Anthony was putting in extra effort to cheer me up lately but it was barely working. I was worried constantly. Something in Maria's eyes tells me she has a plan, I just don't know what it is.

I feel like I am constantly living in fear.

"I found another tile that's off kilter," Mr. Bryne told us that evening in the room.

"Where?" I asked.

"In the place that would have been Marcus's room. I am reading his journal and Maria's side by side. His tells me he was very disturbed and was being bullied by someone or something. I think it is Maria," he said quietly.

"We will take a look at it and try to get whatever is inside out," Christian replied.

Everyday Maria became more of her true self. She was no longer pretending to be a good ghost anymore. We started searching desperately for more clues, with or without her watchful eyes.

The Legion watched me carefully and was always around

me. Something made me feel like they wanted to talk to me but they were scared of Maria.

I took them into our room and closed the door, so it was just us.

"Maria has gotten access to some kind of power that she was not supposed to have. She summoned us and bound us with her blood when she was alive. We should have been able to leave when she died but she somehow bound us to the house. When Marcus came, she possessed him, and then bound us to him. Now that she has been released from her prison, she is looking for Marcus. You will need to find him first. If she finds him before you do, she will yield full power over us. Thank you for your audience." They bowed to me and moved toward the door.

I left them out of the room and stayed inside, locking the door.

I brought out all the journals that Marcus had written in. He obviously wanted someone to find him, leaving clues so we could. I just had to decipher his hidden messages to find him.

I laid each journal out according to the year he wrote them. He journaled every year for six years. I arranged them in that order.

There was a knock on the door.

"Who is it?" I asked, knowing that Maria could pretend to knock.

"It's us," Anthony responded.

I open the door, letting them in quickly.

"What are you doing?" Christian asked.

"The Legion had an audience with me. They told me something interesting about Maria." I proceed to fill them in on everything.

"So I have all of Marcus's journals laid out in order. About ten pages are missing from the end of each journal, except the first one. It is complete." I explained to everyone.

"What kind of power does Marcus have over the Legion that Maria wants? She pretty much controls them now as it is," Damien said.

"Maria is power hungry. She has some kind of sick ambition to take a human body and make herself popular. She wants to rule the world. I got information on her death and it was not pretty. She was brutally killed but it was her boyfriend's wife that killed her. She was dating a politician who was married. His wife put an end to his life when she found out that Maria was been pregnant. She's full of vengeance because she felt like she didn't yield enough power to protect her life and she wants to avenge that. She knew she was going to be killed. That is why she put all of this in place. She is very dangerous," Mrs. Bryne said.

We prepared a plan on how to find Marcus and his hidden pages.

MARIA

They have been trying to outsmart me and I am losing my grip on the Legion. But it won't be for long, I will get Marcus soon. I can feel it.

"What are they planning?" I asked the Legion.

"We cannot hear them, remember?" they responded.

"You all are useless. Get out of my sight!" I shouted and walked away.

I paced around the house and then I saw her. I could feel her desperation and I could see a lot of me in her. She could be my ticket to accomplishing my goals.

She loved the house as much as I loved it and that made me happy.

She will be perfect for me.

At least for now.

I smiled.

ANTHONY

"That tile won't move," Lucien complained.

"I don't think we should blasting it. We just need a way to break the tile," my father said.

"I don't think we should just break it. We don't know what is under there and we don't need to damage whatever it is," I replied.

"I think we can drill it and not cause much damage," Damien suggested.

"That is actually a good idea but where do we find a drill?" Mr. Martini asked.

"I will ask Mom," Christian went to the room to find Mother.

Mother followed Christian back into the room. "Let me look at this before you start destroying things."

We found that we had to move the tiles around like a puzzle to open it.

Lucia did the puzzle and opened it. There was a satchel left in the ground. We brought it out and found a bottle.

After hours of examining the bottle, we still could not make sense of it. It was glued shut and refused to open.

After a while, Lucia spoke up, "I think Marcus is trapped inside the bottle. That's why it is so hard to open."

"If it is truly Marcus, then we cannot allow Maria to see the bottle. She knows exactly how to get him out," Mrs. Bryne said.

"I don't think it is because if Marcus wanted to stay away from Maria in a place she could not find him, do you think it would be wise enough for him to hide in a bottle? And who sealed the floor shut?" Lucien asked.

"That makes sense. So, what is this bottle for?" Lucia asked and the room fell silent again.

Christian took the bottle and read the cap. It was similar to Latin.

"I have heard that saying before," Mother said as she took the bottle and looked at it carefully. "It is a puzzle. I need a pen and paper," Mother looked very excited.

She took the paper and quickly wrote down the wordings, then she turned it around and stared at it for a while.

She smiled at us and continued writing.

"Red, blue, black," she said quietly and the bottle opened up.

We all stood there in shock. "How did you know this trick?" I asked.

"A ghost taught me of it once. She said it was a common spell that was used a lot in the 1800s," Mother enlightened us.

"Okay, so what is inside the bottle?" Mrs. Martini appeared eager to get whatever was in the bottle out.

It was the last part of Marcus's journal.

Lucia brought out all of the journal's and arranged them properly, they all fit. She sat down on the floor, starting to read the last pages of the journals.

"Finally, we are close to finding Marcus or learning the truth," Lucien rejoiced.

"They are a continuation of each other. This is about Maria. The real Maria!" Lucia said excitedly.

That night we stayed up reading through every journal, finding out the truth. It got scarier with every new page.

She tortured Marcus, making him go crazy. The last few

paragraphs he wrote described how to capture Maria and how to send the Legion back. He stated that the Legion had to be sent back before Maria or they will remain trapped in this house forever. He clearly wrote the spells and the steps involved to capture her.

We put everything back into the bottle and we hid it.

"Okay, we need to set up a plan," I said to everyone and we spent the next few hours discussing how we would send Maria and the Legion to the afterlife and how we needed to find Marcus before Maria did.

When we went out for dinner, the house felt odd. It felt like Maria was conspiring. We could not see her around and she didn't come to disturb us as usual.

Something feels different.

I looked around as I tried to figure out what was wrong.

"Lucia, where is your mother?" I asked as I noticed Mrs. Martini was missing.

"She is upstairs. She wanted to get a shawl because she was feeling cold," Lucia responded.

"I think something is wrong. Maria is nowhere to be seen. Your mother should not be alone," I said just as we heard a piercing scream.

We ran upstairs and saw Maria hovered over Lucia's mother, who was trembling from fear.

"Leave her alone!" my mother said.

"Why? We both want the house. It is only fitting we become one," she smiled coldly.

"Leave my mother alone!" Lucia shouted and ran towards them but Maria sent her flying the other way with her hand.

My heart raced as Lucia's body hit the ground. I tried to race to the other side of the room where Lucia was but Maria used her powers on me and I found myself hitting the railing outside the room. Pain coursed through me.

My family ran towards me to check if I was okay. I nodded even though I was sure that I had broken a rib or two, making it difficult for me to breathe.

"Please help me. Don't let her possess me," Mrs. Martini cried out. Maria laughed as she started moving around Mrs. Martini.

 # LUCIA

"Ugh," I groaned as I held my head.

My mother cried out for help. Maria started spinning around her so she could get her bearings and flow into my mother's body.

I had to do something to stop her.

But what could I do?

Then I remembered one article I had read when we first came to the house.

It said that we could use our bodies as physical traps for ghosts. If I could just remember the chant I am supposed to say, I could help her.

In panic, I slit my wrist and started moving in a circle. Maria was immediately attracted to my blood and rushed towards me. I trapped her in the circle of my blood and I started chanting what I had read, hoping it would work.

I entered into the circle with her and I screamed as she moved around me. I felt a piercing pain as a bond formed between us. I could not stop the pain or stop the tears from pooling in my eyes.

"Lucia!" I heard my mother scream, but I could not turn to look at her. I felt my body fall to the ground as I convulsed. Maria tried to fight me in my body. She tried to take control but I didn't allow her.

I slit my other wrist and watched the blood pour out of

my artery. I laid down and felt life drain from my body. I found myself in stark darkness.

"Why did you do that?!" Maria shouted at me.

"I will never allow you to harm my parents," I looked at her smugly.

"Ha, foolish child. There is something you need to know. You made sure we were trapped together, but you have forgotten my abilities. It looks like you also didn't remember I was trapped for centuries. Trust me I can out wait you. At the end of the day, I will accomplish my mission," she gripped my throat. "You don't know what you started, little girl. You may end up regretting it," she laughed.

I looked at her, pretending to be scared. I walked up to her and she became tense. "You don't know how far a girl who has tried multiple times to take her life will go. I am scared of nothing and let me remind you that I will end you in multiple ways," I laughed like I had gone crazy.

I saw a streak of light at a distance. I tried to walk towards it but she tried to pull my hands back.

I turned to look at her. "Don't touch me."

I continued to move forward and I know she followed.

"I know you like to see me as the bad person but do you know what they did to me? You know nothing about me except what Marcus wrote and the few things you probably researched. Do you know how I had to fight to survive? Yes, I summoned the Legion, I slept with a married man and I killed my bastard baby. I made Marcus mad and I possessed him a couple of times to do my bidding. But that is nothing compared to the torture I had to endure. That is nothing compared to what those people did to me!" she shouted as tears pooled at the corner of her eyes.

I wanted to feel sorry for her but I remembered that she was old and had been a ghost for very long time. She had learned the act of manipulating people to believe what she wanted them to believe.

"Why should I believe you? Why should I trust what you say?" I walked closer to the light.

"Because you know what it feels like to be oppressed. I know you have been assaulted. I understand why your only interests are dangerous things and writing. I know why you started writing," she moved closer to me and I saw myself in her eyes.

I saw myself trapped in that life, constantly manipulated and assaulted by Miguel.

"Get the fuck away from me!" I shouted as I pushed her away.

She brought it back, the memories I tried to forget. I was foolish when I decided to move to Mexico at sixteen to live with my grandmother. I met Miguel who was twenty-four and let him into my life. I mistook whatever he felt for love, but as I got older, I realized he only used me because being with me benefited him. He never cared for once how what he was doing could affect me. If I complained about what he was doing, he would make his friends make me pay. It was two years before I was able to break free from him and come back to the States. I never talked to anyone about it. I couldn't even tell my therapist why I was depressed.

Now Maria tried to use it to bond with me.

"I am not trying to bring back the memories, I am just telling you what I experienced. Do you know what it took to be a singer back then. Do you think we were appreciated the way women are appreciated now? Back then, if you were a female singer, you might as well have gone naked on the streets and claimed you were a brothel worker. I was made a sex slave for months, just to get gigs. When I finally started getting good enough gigs to make me good money, my manager Charlie made sure to take every penny from me. You may think I am just fabricating lies to try to bond with you but I think it's time you start seeing me for what I am."

She held out her hands to me and decided to take me through her life journey. "I will make sure you see what made me what I am today," Maria held my hand and took me into her life memories.

MARIA

I know she put me inside her body to cage me but I needed her to trust me. She had to see where I was coming from and what was pushing me to make such decisions.

I cannot let everything I have waited for leave me like that.

I was trapped in that house for centuries. I will not let this little girl trap me again.

I will show her what she wants to see, if that means I will get to accomplish my mission.

ANTHONY

We got the pain Lucia was in to ease and her heart rate had returned to normal. I think it was from us. Her mother has been crying the whole time. I know that we have to look for Marcus's trapped ghost to find a way to remove Lucia from whatever trap she made for Maria.

"Anthony, bring those journals. There must be something there that will point to where Marcus is," Mother said to me.

"But it is possible that Marcus is in the afterlife," Lucien said.

"Shut up," I growled before realizing I had no right to be angry with him.

"Why have you been acting like something crawled up your ass and died? We were all here when Lucia sacrificed herself and I can tell you we are all affected," Damien said to me.

"You don't understand. There is a possibility that Lucia may not come out from that cage she trapped herself and Maria in. She may also come out and not be able to continue her life normally. She is already dealing with depression. I cannot allow anything more to happen to her. If we had worked better, or been more careful, she wouldn't have been IN that situation." Tears pooled in my eyes as guilt ate me up.

Damien enveloped me in a hug. He understood what I was going through without explaining it to him. I suddenly started to doubt myself and I felt like I was the problem. I should have done better. This is the same thing that happened to Isabel. I led her to her death and now I am doing the same with Lucia.

"Stop blaming yourself, it was not your fault. If you want to cast blame, we all had a fault in this. We caused this upon ourselves one way or another." Damien consoled me but I felt anything but consoled.

The air became chilled again and distorted figures started to appear from different places.

It was the Legion.

"What are you doing here?" Mother asked.

"We are the Legion and we are here to see Lucia. Where is she?" they asked, their voices echoing through the room.

"She is laying on the bed. She made herself a human trap for Maria," Father responded and they looked over to Lucia. They looked almost sympathetic.

"Do you know where Marcus is? You must have helped Maria to trap Marcus," I walked up to them.

"We may have an idea but we are not sure. When we found out what Maria was planning, we warned Marcus. We are not sure if he is trapped or in the afterlife, but we can follow you around the house. If we feel his energy, then he is still here and we can find him," the Legion replied to me.

That was not enough. We needed to be sure of where Marcus was. We could not continue like this. As more time went by, with the trap Lucia used to trap Maria we may not be able to bring her out.

"Let us start checking the house," Mrs. Martini quickly stood up and the Legion went along with her. We followed.

We walked around the house, but it was large and we could not go everywhere at once.

When everyone went to sleep, I took out Marcus's journals and I went through all of them again.

We must be missing something.

There must be something that shows where Marcus is trapped.

I went up to the attic, to the deserted altar that Maria made. I saw a brownish book situated at the back of the altar and I opened it.

"Maria" was written there.

I realized that these were her true journals. I took everything out and went to the room, opening all of them and reading through them.

By the time dawn came, I could not believe what Maria was. She was truly a terrible person and I was more alarmed because Lucia was trapped with her and only God knows what she could be telling Lucia right now.

"Anthony," Mother called as she walked downstairs.

"Yes, Mom," I replied, not taking my eyes off the book.

"You didn't sleep, did you?" she asked and I shook my head.

"You have to rest. You cannot continue like this, you will cause serious injuries to yourself."

"Mom, I will not be able to live with myself if I don't find a way to bring Lucia back. I cannot let her be a human cage for Maria," I rubbed my temples repeatedly.

"You are in love with her," my mother stared into my eyes.

"What?" I chuckled.

"You are in love with Lucia, Anthony," Mother said.

I burst out laughing.

"Why would you say that? I am simply feeling guilty because we were hired to protect them from situations like this and instead, we let her be a human cage for one very deadly ghost," I replied.

"You may not believe it and you may try to lie to yourself but you know in your heart what I am talking about. You are feeling this miserable not only because you failed to protect her but because you are in love with her. When you are ready to talk, I am here for you," Mother said and got up from the chair.

I stared blankly at the wall for a very long time as I thought about what Mother said.

Is it possible that I had stopped loving Isabel somewhere along the line and Lucia had taken over my heart?

Is it possible that I am so miserable because I am in love with her?

But the way I feel about her is different from the way I felt about Isabel.

MARCUS

I could see them. I could hear their conversations. If only they could see me and hear me and see that I am calling out to them.

Maria is way more dangerous than they all know and those journals, even the one she wrote by herself, does no justice to what she really did.

I saw Lucia's hand move and I am sure that Maria is poisoning her mind slowly, trying to make her wake up so she can continue her deeds. She saw me, she saw me before she was trapped. She needed a human body to release me from this trap, so she wanted to possess Mrs. Martini.

All I want to do is go home.

I am tired.

I want to rest.

I need to put in more effort to reach out to Anthony.

LUCIA

Maria took me back to when she was little and running through the streets of Seattle in the 1600s. Her parents had been poor but she always had the dream of being a singer, even though her mother advised her it would be better for her to be a trader. Her father beat her for going to singing gigs.

At age sixteen, Maria ran away from the house and that was the first time she was sexually assaulted. A kind looking man named Robert asked her to follow him so that she could be his maid and be able to get some money. She agreed but she didn't notice the vicious look on his face.

He took her to his large home where he already had plenty of maids and placed her in the kitchen as the cook's assistant.

The cook didn't like her and treated her sternly. "He got in your panties, didn't he?" the cook spat disdainfully.

Maria did not understand what she meant and she told the cook that but that only made the woman smack her head with the wooden spatula she was using to stir the soups.

"Don't lie to me little girl. That is what you young girls do to get jobs in high places nowadays. A girl like you should be in a maiden school, and if your parents are too poor to send you to one, you should be in a tailoring shop, learning to sew dresses," the woman accused.

Maris stared at her blankly and she didn't know what to

say. She told the lady how she met the good sir and he told her he will help her have a better life.

All the servants heard this and laughed. For some reason, they hated her and treated her poorly.

One night, the man called her to his room and she went without thinking of anything. The man dragged her into the room and began to kiss her and touch her in places that her mother always told her was forbidden for a man to touch.

She pleaded with the man to let her go. He asked her if the kindness he showed her was for free.

She told him she didn't understand what he meant and he responded to her saying, "Nothing goes for nothing."

Then he tore her clothes open and raped her.

Maria ran out of the house. She lived on the streets for a while before she begged a tailor to take her in and train her. The mistress was kind to her and taught her all she needed to know about tailoring, paid her a good salary, and even clothed her.

She stayed with the tailor for about two years before the shop folded and she was forced to leave.

Throughout her life she faced hardship and at the age of twenty-two, she became a bartender. She worked at the bar and sometimes she was offered gigs.

Charlie came in one night and saw her singing. He immediately introduced himself to her and told her he wanted to help her sing. That night, she resigned from her job and agreed to join the man.

She was not literate and did not read the deal when she signed it.

She was forced to sleep with rich men and senators in the gathering where she went to sing. Charlie abused her but her voice was very good. Soon she started getting high paid gigs but she did not get the money because Charlie collected all of it.

There was something strange about her story. She took me through all her memories and I knew she experienced a lot of bad things but I knew what we experienced was not the same. She removed all of the good things that happened to her and just showed me the bad things and some lies too. At first, I wanted to believe her and my resolve had started to soften. I would have released her from the cage but then I started spotting the loop holes in her story.

"This is not real," I said to her. She turned around to face me as I removed my hand from hers.

"What do you mean by that?" she asked furiously.

"I said it is not real. The memories you are trying to tell me have a lot of loopholes. Some of them must have really happened to you but there are also lies in there. You are trying so hard to relate to me so you can leave," I spoke fiercely.

Her eyes turned red and she moved towards me with rage and hatred emitting from her.

"I will not let you stop me! I will kill you before that happens. I am so close to getting what I want and you will not sabotage it for me," she held on to my neck and lifted me from the ground.

I clawed at her hand trying to detach it from my neck as my vision started to get dark spots.

ANTHONY

We still haven't made any progress and time is running out. I started to get the feeling that I was being watched but when I looked around, I didn't see anyone. I knew deep down someone was watching me.

Lucia began to convulse. I rushed towards her and tried to calm her but I knew whatever was happening to her was being caused by Maria.

"What is going on?" Mrs. Martini asked with fear written all over her body.

"Maria is fighting her. She is trying to take control of Lucia's body and she is resisting," Damien responded.

"We need to find Marcus and fast," I added quietly.

"I am right here," I heard somebody whisper.

I turned and looked around.

Who said that?

"Did you guys hear that?" I asked them.

"Hear what?" Lucien questioned. They had managed to calm Lucia down and she wasn't convulsing anymore.

"Somebody said I am right here," I answered.

"Okay, there is something going on with you. You need to rest," Damien said.

"No, I don't need to rest. I am telling you that I heard something." I stood firmly.

"You are tired and this issue is stressing you out. Nobody said anything," Damien insisted.

"I am not tired." I shoved past Damien, who held my hand.

"Where are you going?" he asked.

"You don't need to know," I started walking away when something caught my eye.

It was a shadow but it was faint, very faint, almost invisible to the eyes.

I walked towards it. As I got closer, I saw the silhouette of a man.

That was Marcus. I was so sure.

"Marcus?" I called out.

"Yes, I am here. I am locked underneath this tile," I heard him say. Then it occurred to me that Marcus was talking inside my head.

"Damien, the drill!" I shouted to my brother who quickly brought the drill.

I drilled the tile and opened it up to find a skull and a little box.

I brought it out and found out it had a lock.

"Let me," Mother collected the box from me and took a pin from her hair to open up the box.

She turned the pin in different angles and then we heard the click sound and Marcus burst out of the box.

"Finally!" He shook his ghostly body.

"We need to find a way to get Maria out of Lucia's body," I rushed out before he could say anything.

"We will do that, but first we need to take the Legion out of this place. We need to send them to the afterlife. If I help you free Maria from her human cage, and the Legion and I are still here, then none of you will be saved. She has a lot of anger and vengeance in her heart and that is what is driving her but don't be deceived. She is responsible for everything that happened to her despite whatever lies she must have told you. She has powers she hasn't used yet and is waiting for the right time. I don't think anybody has survived her fury," Marcus enlightened us.

"You will tell us all about Maria later, but first you need to show us how to send the Legion out of this house. We are running out of time," I interrupted him.

"Okay, first you need twenty-seven candles and beach sand. I will show you how to line them in circles and ancient writing. You will also need a portal to the afterlife and your blood." Marcus said.

"Okay, we will do it tonight. I will drive to the beach to get the sand and you will get the candles." I pointed to Damien.

Then I walked out of the house and almost sobbed in joy that I will finally have my Lucia back.

What the hell am I saying?

"Oh, shut up!" I groaned and continued my drive to the beach.

I got the beach sand and then went back home.

When I got back, I noticed that Damien had arrived. We lit all the candles on the floor and I started drawing the little circles that Marcus showed me.

"Each circle is for each Legion and so is the candle," he explained.

"Now put the bowl in the middle, cut your hands, and let the blood drop into the bowl," Marcus told us and we did exactly as he said.

"Move gently in circles and recite after me," he instructed and we followed.

When we finished chanting, a sharp breeze came from nowhere and the lights flickered off, leaving only the candle lights on.

Then the Legion began to come out with their distorted bodies and they stood in their circles. Then Mother opened up the portal and they all left one by one into the afterlife.

MARIA

I could feel Marcus's presence and I knew they had found him.

I started fighting harder with Lucia to take charge of her body.

Who knew a depressed little girl like this would be so strong?

We struggled for hours and I felt the Legion go back into the afterlife. I realized what Marcus was helping them do.

They wanted to take my powers away but they didn't know what drove me.

I increased my struggle with Lucia because it looked like she was growing stronger by the minute.

We continued to go back and forth until I became too tired. and I decided to try to use my powers on her, but it could cause more trouble for me.

Either I am sent to the afterlife or she is.

ANTHONY

After we sent the Legions to the afterlife, we went upstairs to the room to see Lucia writhing on the floor.

"Maria is draining her. We have to act fast," Marcus said as he quickly ran towards Lucia. "We need to make a circle around her, quickly!" Marcus shouted and we all surrounded Lucia.

He started saying some ancient words and the more he spoke, the more Lucia convulsed.

"What is going on?" Mrs. Martini cried.

"You are going to have to trust me," Marcus said as he continued chanting and moving around in circles.

Lucia's convulsion got more violent but then she started slowing down. When she opened up her eyes, Maria flew out of her.

Marcus clasped his hands and Maria was suspended on air.

"That will hold her temporarily. You need to send me to the afterlife now, while someone burns up her altar," Marcus said. I quickly ran upstairs and set fire to the altar in the attic, making sure that everything got burned while the rest sent Marcus to the afterlife.

Maria looked mad. She looked like she was about to unleash her fury. We knew she could not do so much now that Marcus and the Legion were gone. We were so wrong.

Maria screamed as soon as she was released. She screamed

like a banshee. It was so loud that we all fell to the ground in pain.

"Maria!" Lucia shouted as she held her ears and blood pooled from her nose.

Maria smiled and suddenly disappeared. We carried Lucia to the room where we placed the Teflon to stop Maria from entering.

"We need to find a way to get rid of Maria. Leaving her here is dangerous," my mother said before she led the others out of the room.

I couldn't care about anything she was saying. All my focus was on Lucia and how she was behaving.

"What's wrong?" I asked Lucia.

"I don't know. I can still feel Maria inside me, her essence is inside me," she spoke quietly to me.

"What?" I almost shouted. "What do you mean? Like she is still inside you and she wasn't completely removed or you can feel remnants?" I asked.

"Yes, there are remnants of her inside me." Lucia nodded.

Fuck this is not good.

All the alarm bells in my head were ringing.

"Try to get some sleep. We will talk about this with everyone in the morning," I told her.

I hoped all would be well and whatever essence of Maria she felt, would be cleared in the morning.

 # LUCIA

I was scared.
It felt like she was still lingering in me, waiting for me to be alone before she strikes. It is a good thing that I am never alone and we all stay together to avoid her.

"You know you can never escape me. You never will." She laughed as she reached out to me and took my hand in hers. "You will help me become great," she smiled at me.

"No!" I screamed and I opened my eyes to see everyone around me, asking me what was going on.

"I... no... Maria," I tried to form actual words but nothing I said was going to make sense.

Then I saw her. She entered the room and waved at me.

She smiled and floated back out.

"Maria," I pointed towards the door.

"What are you saying? No one is there," My mother said.

"You all didn't see her?" I asked as I shuddered.

"No, we didn't see anyone," Mrs. Bryne replied.

"I think Maria left her essence in Lucia and she is trying to make her lose her mind," Anthony said angrily.

"What? That is impossible!" my mother said.

"It's not impossible. It is happening, Mom."

Tears fell from my eyes.

"We need to find a way around this," Lucien said and they all consoled me and we went back to sleep. I was disturbed terribly by the dreams I kept having. They were not good.

Maria kept interrupting whatever good dream I was having. Eventually, I gave up trying not to see her in my dreams and actually embraced the fact that she was showing up.

THREE WEEKS HAVE PASSED and the tormenting did not stop. She kept on interrupting my sleep and I always woke up feeling exhausted and less enthusiastic in the morning.

With time, I started to wonder why was I living.

I was becoming more and more depressed and everything seemed to look gray. I didn't like the life I was living and there was nothing I could do about it.

I could not change it.

I had to continue living like this and it freaked me out that Maria would always be a part of my life.

On some days, life felt better because Anthony was there to cheer me up and other days, it looked plainly gray. I cried myself to sleep most times and hoped nobody would notice. I doubled my dose on my anti-depressants and it still didn't give me any effect. It was still the same. It still made me feel sad and unenthusiastic and I started thinking about dying more often.

The world suddenly became too much and I could not take it anymore. I didn't want to live here anymore. I was constantly tired and just wanted to rest.

"Lucia," Anthony called me, shaking me out of my thoughts.

"What are you doing here all by yourself and what are you thinking about?" he asked me.

"Nothing much. I am just thinking about how life would have been without me seeing Maria everywhere. The fact that she hasn't appeared and none of you are seeing her except for me, it shows that she is bent on torturing me and making me crazy," I said to Anthony, who was suddenly looking angry.

Maria didn't care about his fury. All she cared about was tormenting me, and deep down I knew why.

Everyone was talking about how Maria has disappeared from our lives but I could see her in every corner I looked. Like she was there watching me and mocking me, waiting for me to make a mistake and laugh at me.

One night, she was struggling with me over my body and I asked her, "Maria, why? Why are you tormenting me?"

And she gave me the simplest and most honest answer, "Because I can."

MARIA

It was fun to see Lucia being so jumpy, but after a few weeks, I was getting tired of her. I wanted to do something to all of them.

I wanted my chances back. They looked like they were happy and that is what I wanted. I will come back stronger and with more wrath, but I wanted to break Lucia first.

Scaring her made me feel some kind of satisfaction and that is all that mattered.

Since the Legion has gone, I decided to call on every kind of malevolent spirit I could find, but they were busy. The ones that weren't busy wanted a price too high to pay.

I decided it was time to pay a visit to my old friend in the underworld.

"Hello, Manuel," I smiled as I moved seductively and walked towards him. I felt his breath quicken and that made me giggle.

"Hey, sugar, long time," he smiled at me.

"I was hoping you would be available." I smiled.

"What do you need? You know I cannot refuse you anything." He smiled and that made me feel more important.

"I need your most violent spirits. I want to torture some humans and possibly kill them, if I am feeling nice. I will probably do what I did to Marcus." I giggled thinking about it.

"What happened to Marcus? I haven't heard from him in a long time," Manuel questioned.

"The humans I want to torture helped free him from my terror and they also unbounded me from the Legion. Now I am thinking of ways to make their lives miserable. I have already started with the girl, Lucia. She thought she could use her body as a human cage for me. Brave little girl. I will continue to torment her until she is forced to take her own life," I smiled at him.

"Good to see you haven't changed. That is wonderful. I have a set of spirits that work like the Legion, they are called Malevolent. They are filled with anger and will stop at nothing until they have accomplished their mission. They don't torment. Instead, they kill without mercy. They can possess these human and make them turn against each other. They can cause a human to want to kill their family," Manuel enlightened me on his new toys.

"I will take them," I smiled with mischief.

"What will I get in return?" he asked seductively.

I felt a tinge of disgust go through my body but I have learned sometimes you have to take shortcuts to get to the top.

Nobody would know about them later.

"I am here at your service, Manual," I smiled.

"Good girl," he laughed.

ANTHONY

Every day I could feel Lucia pulling away. She didn't want to be involved in anything that was going on.

All she wanted was to be left alone. Sometimes she would hold her head and scream and other times she would leave the house, not showing any sign of coming back.

It looked like we were losing her slowly no matter what we did and that made me feel pain in my heart.

I have lost the woman I loved once, I will not let it happen again.

"Lucia," I called out to her as she returned.

"Hi," she said weakly.

"Where did you go to hide?" I asked her with a teasing smile.

"Don't look at me like that. I went to the park at the other side of town," she smiled at me.

"Okay." I looked down at her.

"Do you like baking?"

"Of course," she nodded eagerly.

Good, I have gotten her attention.

"What is your favorite thing to bake?" I asked her.

"Chocolate chip cookies," she giggled like a child, while she told me about her fond memories baking chocolate chip cookies.

"You sound like a real naughty child," I teased.

"I was a real naughty child." She winked.

We walked to the kitchen, and we brought out all the ingredients for a chocolate chip cookie.

"Taste the dough." She lifted the dough to my lips.

"No thank you. I prefer to taste the chocolate chip, better still the cookies." I laughed.

"You have to do a taste test to know if the dough is right or you will make the worst chocolate chip cookies of your life." She laughed.

"Why do I feel like there is a memory there?" I squinted my eyes at her.

"Don't look at me like that. I am hiding nothing. There is a memory there and it is not one I am willing to share." She shrugged.

"Tell me now or I will turn into the tickle monster and make sure you tell me!" I came closer to her and she squealed.

"No!" she shouted as I started to tickle her.

"Wait, wait. I'll tell you!" She laughed until tears came out from her eyes.

Seeing her like this brought joy to my heart.

As we continued baking the cookies, she told me her story. "One day, we were baking the cookies and I used salt instead of sugar. That's when my mother told me that you always taste the dough so you don't waste time baking bad batches."

"No, really?! That would have been a shock to the taste buds!"

AFTER WE FINISHED BAKING the cookies, we ate them with milk while we chatted. I looked upstairs to see my mother smiling down at us.

# LUCIA

The past few days have passed by in bliss. Anthony has been so sweet and Lucien is just so funny. He makes me come with him to the front of the house where he does his research and he cracks me up all day. Many people don't know the kind of comedian he is, even his family. He is a jester. Normally, I would smile in thought of it. But not today.

Today is not so good.

I feel mentally drained. Thinking about my life and how it has taken a turn, it is too much. Maria's visits were no longer as frequent as they used to be but I felt like I had been holding on for so long. I let myself think about my life before I came to this show and I realized I have always been broken.

For the first time since I came to this house, I allowed myself to feel and think about everything that has happened so far. I allowed myself to feel and I am very depressed. I don't feel like leaving my bed today and my door is locked.

I can't help but contain unwanted thoughts. I thought about my antidepressants, which I have doubled the dose, but it still does nothing for me.

Do I really want to be involved with all of this?

I am thinking of what happened between Berry, Madeline, and every ghost I have encountered and for the first time I don't care. I really think it has nothing to do with me.

I want to sleep for a long time.

I feel like I am drowning and I need a breath of fresh air.

I haven't slept well for days and the thought of seeing Maria in my dreams makes me stay up late.

I keep on getting flashes of how life has always felt for me. How I have never truly been happy. Tears roll down my cheeks, and I let myself be sad. There is something about sadness and depression. It draws you into its comfortable dark shadows and it clouds your entire being and for a moment you are one with the pain and darkness and it starts feeling too comfortable and very soon you become addicted to it and you don't know how to exist without the pain anymore.

I lay on my bed and sigh for the hundredth time as tears clouds my vision. I am truly tired and I question myself again.

Is it truly worth it?

Is being alive and fighting through all of this worth it?

Was I truly scared of going outside after it took me an entire year to get over that fear?

I lay in bed all day thinking about my life. At exactly seven o'clock at night, the flashes suddenly become too much.

The pain too unbearable.

All I want is silence but instead I see silhouettes, making me question what I see.

I need peace and quiet. So I do the first thing that comes to mind.

I go into my bathroom and I turn on the water in the bathtub. I climbed in with my clothes on, not feeling the need to take them off. I felt too weak to do so. I lay in the tub and I closed my eyes.

I feel peace for the first time today.

Finally, I don't feel Maria's essence.

I don't feel anybody's presence, all I feel is me. I should have been scared. I should have thought about how any spirit, or even Maria, could appear and try to choke me as I laid down in this bath tub. But I did not think of any of any of that. I took deep breaths as the water got higher and I sink in deeper. Soon I am submerged in the water as it flows out of the tub, but I don't care. All I care about now is the peace.

I paused taking in the serenity, the way it looks so beautiful but too good to be true. The way there is nothing really serene about my life. The way my life is chaotic but for this moment I can pretend that everything is fine.

Is that what I really want?
Is that why I am here?

No one is here to watch me or try to cheer me up, or give me the strength to try to act happy, or peaceful or calm.

So, I do the one thing my life makes me feel like doing all the time.

I scream.

I scream my lungs out.

I scream that I have no control over my life right now and how I have had no control for a very long time.

I scream because after I thought everything was beginning to get so much better, and it suddenly became so much worse. After I thought this would be my new beginning, it got scarier. Now I was more scared to dream or be myself. I could not write or do anything I loved because I was constantly in fear. I can't help but sob. I feel the sobs from my soul and I start to fight but I feel weaker and my vision starts to become black and I remember, there is nothing to fight for and I let myself sleep.

Finally, I'd get peace.

ANTHONY

I was not okay with the fact that Lucia decided to stay home but I told myself not to think too much about it. I practiced what my mother has always taught me, hope for the best because everything is possible with faith.

I felt uneasy and everything in me was pushing me to go back home, to the point I was no longer enjoying myself and my thoughts were consumed by Lucia.

How is she coping staying by herself at home with no one to cheer her up?

Is she constantly worried that Maria would appear out of the blues at torture her just like she has done weeks before?

Is she scared and hiding under the blanket like I have seen her do recently and looking around to make sure that she is the only person in the house or is she silently crying like she does many nights when she feels as though everyone is asleep?

I couldn't stay calm anymore, so I got up quickly and made my way to the exit.

"Anthony, where are you going?" Damien called out to me.

"Home," I grumbled.

"Why? Are you worried about Lucia? Because she refused to come? I think she just didn't want to come. I know what you are thinking but I can assure you that she is not being tormented right now," Damien tried to make me feel better but I was already very tense and nothing he was doing right now will work unless I see Lucia.

"It is already seven o'clock. We have left her alone for seven hours. For someone who was depressed and is even more depressed and exhausted because of a ghost, it sounds like a suicide mission," I said.

Damien stood thinking about everything I said. "I really don't think she will hurt herself again. I mean she has been laughing a lot lately and she has also been taking her antidepressants. She will be fine." Damien patted my back but I still felt uneasy.

It's true that she has been smiling more lately. but it is due to collective effort between me and Lucien. He has been making her laugh so much lately because I told him about her situation.

"Anthony, what are you doing there? Come here!" Mother dragged me out of my thoughts and with the enthusiasm and all the excitement my family was giving off, I forgot the uneasy feeling in my gut.

"THIS WAS the most fun I have had in a while. I really wish Lucia came with us," Mrs. Martini said to her husband.

We entered the house and it was very quiet. It made me start feeling uneasy again but then I looked at our room and I saw the light was on.

I really hope Maria had not decided to come by after leaving us alone for weeks.

"Lucia, we are home!" her mother called out while we walked into the sitting room.

It was already nine o'clock and we were all exhausted.

"I think she is asleep. It is already kind of late," Mr. Martini said to his wife.

We all talked for about thirty minutes, then we decided to go to bed. We walked to the room to find the door locked.

"Lucia! Come open up the door," her mother said.

"Lucia! Come on, wake up. I am really tired," her mother called out again, but Lucia still didn't answer.

I banged on the door and when we weren't getting any response, I turned to my mother.

"We need to blast this door open!" I spoke with a sense of emergency.

"But that will give Maria and whatever spirits she brings next free access to our room," Christian started to say.

"Who cares? It is a door. We can build another one," I growled as I moved towards my mother.

I positioned the device on the door and we all moved back while the door busted open.

The ground was filled with water and with panicked eyes, I looked on to the bed. There was no sign of Lucia. I rushed to the bathroom and my heart sank when I saw her lying lifeless on the tub.

I ran towards her and got her out of the tub. I noticed her body had turned pale and her pulse was barely there.

She looked lifeless.

I quickly performed CPR on her, while Damien called the ambulance. After a while, I realized they were taking too long and I carried her downstairs into our truck and zoomed off to the hospital.

I didn't care what was going on in the hospital or who needed immediate attention, as I carried Lucia into the ER.

The doctor, who was a family friend, saw how serious the situation was and he took Lucia into the emergency room, where so many different machines were plugged into her body.

"She's had liver failure and we have to perform a surgery

right now. Where are her guardians, husband or family members? We need permission to perform the surgery and we need you to sign some documents," the doctor said.

Lucia's father went to sign the surgery form while my mother consoled her mother.

If I had just stayed at home, none of this would be happening. I should have gone back when I started to feel uneasy but instead I stayed because Damien convinced me to stay.

I should have refused.

The surgery started at midnight and the doctor told us her chance of survival was fifty percent. My heart was in my throat the whole time. I didn't know what to do or where to start from. I sat on the floor of the hospital and silently prayed that she would be alright.

I felt drained.

I didn't want to talk to anybody.

"Anthony, I understand how you must feel. I am sorry." Damien sat beside me but I wasn't ready to answer him.

I did not trust what I would say to him so I kept quiet and just nodded.

"Come on bro," he nudged me.

"Leave me the fuck alone, Damien! This is all your fault. You should have just let me go home. I knew she wasn't happy and I had a feeling in my gut to stay with her. I don't even know why I listened to you and I left her alone. I was foolish to do that and now I am living with my foolishness," I stated.

"You know I didn't intentionally make you stay. If I had known that she would have tried to take her life, if I had known it would be like this, I would not have stopped you from going back home. I thought she was getting better. I didn't know she was putting on a facade," he apologized, but what I needed wasn't an apology.

"Just know that I blame you for what is going on right now." I stood up abruptly and left the room.

I walked for a very long time. I walked aimlessly without direction. She probably tried to kill herself because she felt alone. She didn't have anybody she felt like she could trust to tell them how she really felt.

I should have told her.

I should have told her that I loved her.

Maybe then things wouldn't have been like this, maybe our lives wouldn't have turned out like this. Maybe, just maybe, she would have felt like she could open up to me.

I wallowed in self pity for the rest of the evening and I kept my distance from the hospital.

I kept my distance from her because I felt that I had failed her.

 # LUCIA

Life suddenly felt better and lighter. I haven't felt like this in months, I felt free.

I could not feel Maria's essence anymore.

I didn't feel the need to pretend about my feelings anymore. Here I could be me. The best part of it all is that, I didn't feel any bit of sadness.

I was just floating endlessly, as if going in a direction that I knew nothing about.

Then I thought of him. I thought of the man that has tried his hardest to make me happy .

He paid attention to me and tried to lift my spirits whenever he could.

If I left like this, how will he feel?

I remember when my grandmother died. I remember how helpless I felt. I grieved for months and nobody could console me.

I thought of my parents, especially my mother. She would not be able to console herself, she would never get over it if I just left like that. I could not just leave like that.

If I decide to leave now, Maria will win.

Everything, every single person, soul, spirit or ghost that has hurt me will win. I could not allow that so I did what I know how to do best.

I fought harder.

I went back.
I tried to take my next breath regardless of how I felt.
I will keep on fighting.

ANTHONY

After staying away from the hospital for so long, I went back, and this time I went with a kind of faith that she will be fine. That the Lucia I knew could have weak moments, but she will not stop fighting. I went back to the hospital with one purpose and that was to see her and tell her how I felt. I would not leave her side until I confessed.

Conscious or unconscious.

When I entered the hospital, the doctor came out from her room. I rushed to him immediately as others were already feeling asleep from tiredness.

"How is she now?" I asked.

"She is surprisingly way better. She can now breathe on her own and her heartbeat is now steady. It is a miracle, you know. Many people in her condition don't get better but she is doing well," the doctor said to me.

"Can I see her now?" I asked him hopefully.

"Of course, you can see her. Bear in mind that the patient can hear everything so tell her words of encouragement," the doctor said to me.

I walked into the room and went to her immediately. I held her hand and sat by her bedside.

I didn't know how long she had been out of surgery but I knew she must be very tired. I could not stop the tears that came to my eyes as I saw her in this state.

"I am sorry, my love. I am sorry I was not there for you. I

should not have left you. I should not have left you to be by yourself and I should have told you how much I love you. Yes, we've known each other for a few months and telling you I love you is a little bit too much right now, but I feel you deserve to know. You deserve to know that I love you very much."

I held on to her hand as tears flowed down my cheeks.

I kissed her forehead and left.

MARIA

I came back with my army, the Malevolent.

What I love about them is that they could form into many bodies at once. They could make multiple figures and attack from different sides and they answered to only me.

Yes, I paid a small price to get them, but I am happy I have them now.

"Hello, guys, did you miss me?" I called out as I came into the house.

To my greatest disappointment, nobody was around. The house smelled gravely of death. I giggled as I thought they weren't here because one of them had died.

It would most likely have been Lucia, anyways.

I needed to be back. I needed a body if I was going to follow through with my plans. I know for sure that they can't tell what is coming for them and that alone makes me feel jolly.

I laughed at myself.

 # LUCIA

He loves me.

I heard him confess to me, he loves me.

If I had any doubt about fighting to leave, I guess I just got a lot of motivation.

I thought of Maria and how she would try to torment me or throw me off balance and I laughed.

I laughed because she could not affect me anymore. I was out of her reach and I knew everything. I knew why she acted the way she did, she was insecure. I was scared, and trust me when I say that I will not try to be so good anymore. I will treat her exactly how she needs to be treated.

MRS. MARTINI

We all waited watching Lucia, hoping she would wake up soon.

I can't believe I wasn't there for her again. Just like when she was extremely depressed.

She told us that Maria was around still but we didn't believe her.

Only Anthony did.

"She is awake now," the doctor came out and told us.

I started crying but refused to budge.

"Don't worry. I am sure she is not angry with you and if she was, she has forgiven you," Mr. Martini said to her. "Are you ready to see our baby now?" Mr. Martini asked as he held my hand.

"Yes," I nodded.

We walked into the room and I started crying harder, hugging Lucia and babbling my apology.

"Mother, it's okay. Don't worry, I don't blame you."

Anthony walked into the room and her eyes were trained especially on him.

"Anthony," she called out to him.

When he reached her bedside, I led my husband back out. "Let's give them a bit of privacy."

ANTHONY

When I walked into the room, everyone was staring at me. When she called out to me and I walked to her bedside, they all stood up and left.

"Hi," I whispered as I held her hand.

"Hey," she smiled. "A certain stranger told me he loves me while I was still trying to find my bearings." She smiled at me and I returned the smile.

I wished we could stay in this moment forever, but then I knew it was not possible. We would still have to capture Maria and send her to the afterlife before we could truly be at peace.

"I love you," I moved closer to her and kissed her forehead.

"I love you, too," she responded. I could not stop myself when I leaned in closer and kissed her.

"Please can the rest of the flock come in, love birds?" Christian said, making everyone laugh.

"Of course you can come in," she smiled.

Lucia stayed in the hospital for a few more days while we stayed in the resort. We had not gone back to the house and we didn't know if Maria was back.

When Lucia got released, we took her back to the resort. We already talked about it and we all knew that we could not go back to the house until Lucia was feeling way better.

We spent the next few weeks relaxing and taking family time.

"When are we going back to the house?" Lucia asked one night as we were playing a game.

Everywhere was suddenly quiet as no one knew what to say to her.

"Are you sure you want to go back? I mean we can get a new house. We have been going through this matter for a long time and this is getting old," Mr. Martini said.

"Why? We can go back. I know you are bothered about me but we need to get back at Maria. We need her out of this world. She does not belong here and the world will be better without her," Lucia said.

"Yes, I agree with Lucia. We need to send Maria to the afterlife, she is not meant to be here," I agreed with her.

 # LUCIA

We went back to the house, and it was quiet and eerie. We knew Maria was back because of the chilly feeling.

I could no longer feel her essence in me and I was grateful for that.

As we moved into the house, the light flickered off and we saw different silhouettes making their way around us. First, it was Lucien who screamed, then Damien and Christian. I started to shiver as I felt arms on my hands, and soon, whatever it was dragged me up with so much speed.

I screamed as I found myself hanging upside down beside Christian.

Maria giggled as she snapped her fingers and the lights came on, "Welcome home, sweets," she twirled around the sitting room while her little distorted figure stood and watched her. "Did you miss me? I am back and better." She laughed.

"Why would we miss you? You are nothing but a nuisance and you are not meant to be here. You don't belong here," Mother shouted, her entire face turned red.

"You can say whatever you want but I will stay here for as long as I wish and there is nothing you can do about it."

She winked.

"What did you do to gain your new soldiers?" I asked quietly.

She tensed and she lost her smug demeanor.

"Take her to the room," she said as she turned to leave. "Do you know what? Take all of them to the room, I am done with them."

I laughed. She was miserable and she tried to hide it but I could see the cracks in her.

How could I not see all of these things before?

"What? Why are you laughing?" She faced me, screaming.

"I am allowed to laugh, you know?"

I smiled at her.

"You are insecure," I stated.

"I am not insecure!" Maria screamed and her eyes turned red as she stalked towards me.

I brought out a pendant that I had found in my room. I remembered from the memories she showed me that this was the only thing she still had that reminded her of home.

"Where did you get that?!" she said in a hoarse voice.

"Why are you getting worked up?" I smirked.

Maria yelled, "Leave, quickly, my minions!" She suddenly disappeared, leaving them to follow her.

Where did she go?
She'll be back, we better figure out our plan.

ANTHONY

That evening, we all gathered to talk about how we will expel the new distorted figures Maria came with and send her to the afterlife.

"We need the box that contains that of Maria's heart. That is the only thing that will send her to the afterlife," Mother said.

"Marcus told us that the box is hidden somewhere in the basement. He could have sent her to the afterlife but he went mad shortly after," I said to all of them.

"We need to find it tonight," Christian said.

We searched all night, but we could not find the box and when we decided to retire, Maria appeared.

Her eyes were black and she had this mischievous glint, "Are you looking for this?" she raised a brow.

"The box wih heart," Lucia gasped.

I made a move towards Maria to collect the box but I suddenly felt stuck to the ground.

Soon, it was hard to breathe, it felt like our lungs were constricted.

The entire place was filled with smoke, and the more we struggled, the more it hurt.

Lucien screamed as he tried to move forward and was struck with an intense pain.

"This is your end," Maria laughed as she put the box on the ground and started chanting.

It felt like our insides were contorted as her chants grew louder and it sounded like she was everywhere at once.

Lucia already began to clutch her sides.

Everywhere began to shake and it looked like we were sinking.

My father started moving slowly and we begged him to stop because the more he moved, the more Maria squeezed at his heart.

"I have to get the box of heart, we cannot end like this," Father said.

"Hahaha, fool! You will die before you get to me!" Maria laughed.

Father ignored what she said and he kept on walking forward, even though blood started coming out from his nose.

He finally got his hand on the box of heart and he opened it. A little whirlwind came out.

Suddenly, it felt like Maria's powers started going away as we started to breathe properly and our movements were faster.

"Malevolent, stop them!" Maria shouted, but as her distorted body's moved forward, they were sucked in by the box and then finally, Maria was sucked in.

"No! No! I cannot go down like this!" she screamed.

She stared at us intently and said, "I will be back," as she got dragged into the box.

Father immediately shut the box and covered it up.

Mother opened up the portal, threw the box into the afterlife and the portal closed.

Father held onto his chest and fell to the ground.

"Father!" we shouted in unison as we rushed towards him.

He coughed and spat up blood.

"Ambulance! Call the ambulance!" Mother screamed.

"No, we will drive. It will be quicker," I rushed towards the door as we carried father to the car and drove to the hospital

EPILOGUE

TWO WEEKS LATER

"Thank you, for everything," Mrs. Martini thanked us as we had gotten rid of all the ghosts.

"You are welcome. I can say that we had the most adventurous vacation," Father said from his wheelchair and we all laughed.

"We need to get going," Mother said.

"Wait, there is one more thing I need to do," I said and the lights became dim.

Damien pulled down the curtain and I went down on one kneel.

"Will you marry me, Lucia Martini, and make me the happiest man in the world?"

"Yes, I will marry you," Lucia said with tears in her eyes.

My family members cheered and welcomed Lucia into the family.

join maya black's newsletter

Thank you for reading *The Winchester House, Book One of the Byrne Bloodline!* If you enjoyed it, I'd appreciate you leaving a review anywhere you can!

If you'd like to join my newsletter you can do so at https://www.subscribepage.com/p3j3r1

What do you get? Inside peeks at covers, help choosing characters, what I'm working on next, and so many more fun items!

See you there!

about maya black

Maya Black lives in the Rocky Mountains with her husband and animals and loves being out in nature. She loves all things coffee and books!

She's a new author but has been an avid reader her whole life with stories brewing in her mind. She's finally putting pen to paper to write in a mix of genres but all will include an element of romance.

Join me everywhere you can at https://linktr.ee/authormayablack

also by maya black

STANDALONES

- What Might Have Been
- Yule Spice
- Unchained Melody
- Alice's Illusions
- Wishful Witch
- Bet on Love
- Shallow Beauty
- Rebel Rose
- The Winchester House
- Nick's Wish - November 2025
- Bindings, Crimes, & a Chihuahua (Cozy Mystery) - December 2025

SNOWED IN SERIES

Can be read in any order

- Snowed in with the Mafia
- Snowed in with the Billionaire
- Snowed in with the Brother's Best Friend
- Snowed in with the Professor
- Snowed in with the Coach - December 2025
- More coming in 2026

www.ingramcontent.com/pod-product-compliance
Ingram Content Group UK Ltd.
Pitfield, Milton Keynes, MK11 3LW, UK
UKHW022151151025
8413UKWH00003B/251